W9-BZO-152

You Are My Only

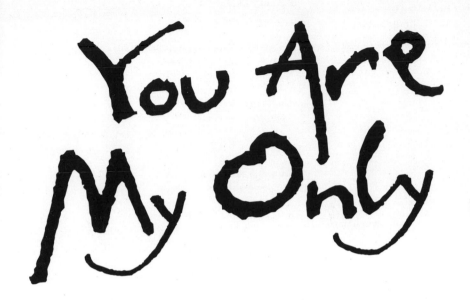

A NOVEL BY

BETH KEPHART

LAURA GERINGER BOOKS

EGMONT
USA
NEW YORK

EGMONT

We bring stories to life

First published by Egmont USA/Laura Geringer Books, 2011
443 Park Avenue South, Suite 806
New York, NY 10016

Copyright © Beth Kephart, 2011
All rights reserved

3 5 7 9 8 6 4 2

www.egmontusa.com
www.beth-kephart.blogspot.com

Library of Congress Cataloging-in-Publication Data

Kephart, Beth.
You are my only : a novel / Beth Kephart.
p.   cm.
Summary: Tells, in their separate voices and at a space of fourteen
years, of Emmy, whose baby has been stolen, and Sophie, a
teenager who defies her nomadic, controlling mother by making
friends with a neighbor boy and his elderly aunts.
ISBN 978-1-60684-272-0 (hardcover) —
ISBN 978-1-60684-285-0 (electronic book)
[1. Mothers and daughters—Fiction. 2. Kidnapping—Fiction.
3. Home schooling—Fiction. 4. Family problems—Fiction.
5. Secrets—Fiction.] I. Title.
PZ7.K438You 2011
[Fic]—dc22
2010052662

Printed in the United States of America

CPSIA tracking label information:
Printed in October 2011 at Berryville Graphics, Berryville, Virginia

For Bill and for Jeremy,
my onlys

Part One

Sophie

My house is a storybook house. A huff-and-a-puff-and-they'll-blow-it-down house. The roof is soft; it's tumbled. There are bushes growing tall past the sills. A single sprouted tree leans in from high above the cracked slate path, torpedoing acorns to the ground.

Splat and crack. Another acorn to the ground.

"Sophie?"

"Mother?"

"I'm off."

"Right."

"Be good."

Be good. My mother's instructions. Her rules.

The floor slats are slants, and the furniture slides, clawing away at the varnish. The walls are pink scratch, or yellow. At the kitchen table, my mother has left my day's work behind—the cardboard from the backs of paper pads, the pencil, the string, the ruler, the hole punch, the dulled-down blade of the old X-Acto knife, the stuff, she says, of an icosahedron. The car door slams, and the engine turns over. The Volvo caroms. The day tilts forward.

Another acorn splats the ground. Another. I climb the long stairs to the third floor, then take the skinny, twisted steps toward the attic. Through the window at the far end falls a milky square of sun, and that's where I'm headed, toward the sun—careful on the crossbeams, careful with the splinters, careful not to fall straight through the quilt of insulation, more scratch, more pink. The window is mine, and the world beyond. They belong to me, my secret.

It's a blue-sky sun day, a puff of clouds. In the patch of yard between my house and the next, a dog is chasing a squirrel into a tree. The squirrel leaps, jumps, climbs the branches toward me, and now a white car with a pistol muffler goes roaring past, down the asphalt road. It disappears, is gone.

A blue truck rides the curve, radio on.

A bird with red tips on black wings flies high.

The dog runs a circle around its tail.

There's the crack of the neighbor's screen door, shoes across the porch, a boy hurrying down the porch steps and around the hedge. He jogs past the garden, to the alley. Tall, he wears his baseball cap turned back around on his head and his belt too loose and long. He calls the dog's name—"Harvey"—and Harvey comes, the sash of his gold tail whipping. The boy holds the dog's snout with one hand and fiddles with a neon ball with the other. Harvey tips onto the back of his paws. When the boy sprints to the end of the alley, his loose belt slaps the air.

Downstairs on the table, beside the salt and pepper shakers, beside the empty butter dish, sits the un-made icosahedron. Outside, through my window, are the boy and the dog, and the boy and the ball, and the boy pitching the ball toward the highest limb of the sprouted tree. The ball falls back down. Harvey snatches it clean. The boy pitches it up and it falls and it is caught in the sharp yellow teeth of the dog.

"Atta dog, Harvey!" the boy says. He runs to collect the ball from Harvey's snout, then runs back the other way. "Here, Harvey!"

My mother is gone. She'll be gone through the morning and the stretch of afternoon and come home tired and sad, rubbing her knees, inquiring after the icosahedron, my math work now as important as all the books I've ever read, from all the libraries in every town we've ever lived, ten of them now, if I were counting. I've kept the stories in my head and the words in books, Kipling's words being some of my favorites. *Greeny-crackly. Fever-trees. Scalesome. Flailsome. Tusky.* I was eight reading those words; I remember. My mother was home, watching the window. "Go to your room," she all of a sudden said, "and shut the door." Just like that, at the height of the Kolokolo Bird adventures. "Stay there—you hear me? Until I tell you to come out." I pretended I didn't hear her. I sat there, reading on. But then she pulled my arm and pointed to the window, and I saw what she had seen—a man advancing on the walk, with a felt hat on his head and a jacket slung over one shoulder. He was carrying a briefcase in one hand.

The No Good, I was sure of it.

"Go," she insisted. And I did.

When the man knocked, she let him in. When he talked, his voice was low and calm. "A child," he was saying. "A proper education . . . state mandated." I got up from the bed, pressed my ear against the door, tried to hear my mother's story, but she was speaking low and waitress calm.

I heard footsteps. I heard back and forth, a rustling of papers, the man's "rules and regulations" and "I'll have someone check the file." Then I heard the opening and closing of the outside door, a good-bye from the man, a good-bye from my mother. "Thank you for coming," she said. "Safe travels."

I pretended to be reading when my mother came to find me. I pretended I'd heard nothing. She didn't say a word. She dragged the closet door across the metal runner until the door snagged in the long hairs of the blue shag carpet and she cursed softly and unsnagged it. She reached to the top shelf that ran along the silver closet bar and pulled the suitcases down, one by one. She undressed the hangers of their blouses and skirts and folded each last thing with air fingers.

"Momma?" I said. "Who was the . . . ?"

"Read your book," she said. "Read it out loud." As if I didn't know what was next, as if this was another bit of nothing.

"'And he caught his tall uncle, the Giraffe, by the hind-leg, and dragged him through a thorn-bush,'" I read, "'and he shouted at his broad aunt, the Hippopotamus, and blew bubbles into her ear when she was sleeping in the water after meals; but he never let any one touch Kolokolo Bird.'" I read, and she undressed the hangers. She air-folded the clothes. She layered them, neatly, into suitcases. We were gone from the house by the next afternoon. We were driving, on the hunt for a better rental. A better library, my mother said. A better job.

"Atta dog, Harvey!" the boy calls, and now when the boy throws the ball, it rises high as my attic window. Rises and rises and falls.

The attic is dust. The insulation is pink. The latch on the window is old-time. I fit my hand to the thing and hear the old lock snap, force the window until the sash breaks away from the sill. The sound, I think, is gunfire, the sound of war. "We live in dangerous times," my mother says. "We must be careful."

The boy tosses the ball and it flies. He tosses again, a

beautiful pitch, and the boy is watching it soar, watching it rise. I lean past the strong arms of the near oak tree, into the day. The ball is falling.

"Hey," I say, and the boy fits one hand above his eyes to visor off the sun. The ball falls and bounces big. Harvey wags his tail and chases the bounce. I watch the boy watching me.

"Play catch?" the boy asks. Just like that.

It's a blue day, a sun day, and the world is out there waiting—the boy. The world is a danger, my mother says, but I will be careful. Careful not to fall between the crossbeams, careful not to slip on the stairs. I find my shoes, fly through the house, undo the locks. There is breeze on my skin. There is the splat of acorns. I cross the porch and turn the corner and there the boy is, smelling like popcorn and laundry. His hair is crooked beneath his cap. I've watched him through my attic window for two weeks and now, today, he sees me.

"I'm Sophie," I say.

He smiles polite, pulls at one ear. "My name is Joey." He steps toward me and I step back, and all of a sudden, Harvey is on me. Harvey—scratch and heat and heavy.

"Down, Harvey," Joey says, but Harvey isn't listening. Harvey's taller than me; he's fur and teeth, dog breath and bark, nothing I can fight against, though I am trying. I hear myself scream and I hear Joey call and I wait for the pain that doesn't come. All of a sudden, the teeth are gone, the fur and the heat and the dog smell.

"Just his way of saying hi," Joey says, his hand in Harvey's collar, his body bent in half, as now he tugs the dog down the alley, past the garden, around the corner, and up the steps, to his front door, moaning and groaning. I hear the screen door slam and Harvey's paws against the door. I hear him yelping. Now, returning, Joey straightens up his pants and fixes his cap, and I straighten, too. I put my hand on my heart to stop it from thumping.

"So you play?" he asks again. "You play ball?"

"Not really," I tell him.

He looks at me hard, and he laughs.

"You live there long?" He thrusts his chin in the direction of my house.

"A couple weeks," I say, running my sneaker over the rough, high grass. "I guess."

"You over at the junior high?" he asks.

"Homeschooled."

"Homeschooled," Joey repeats.

"My mother's a learning fanatic," I tell him.

"I seen her lately," Joey says now. "Down at the diner. Cashier? Black hair? Doesn't talk much? That her? That your mother?"

I nod but don't answer, let Joey look me up and down. "I guess your family isn't big on look-alikes," he says.

"My dad," I say. "I look just like him."

"Where's he at?"

I shrug.

"You don't know where he's at?"

"Never knew him," I say.

"I got it worse," Joey says.

"What do you mean?"

"No mom, no dad. Just two old aunts. You mean you ain't seen 'em?"

"The big one and the little one?" I say. "Yeah. I have. I've seen them." Through my attic window, I've watched his two old aunts come and go—the one built short and round, teacup fashion, pushing the other, skinny as a splinter, in her fancy bamboo wheelchair. "They look too old to be your aunts," I say.

"Aunt Cloris. Aunt Helen," Joey says. "Ain't too bad. We get along."

"That's nice," I say, wishing I was better practiced at conversation.

"So you want to learn catch?" Joey asks.

I nod.

"Come on," he says. "I'll teach you."

"Is it hard?"

"You have two hands?"

I look down at my arms.

"Then hold them out."

"Okay."

"Keep your eye on the ball."

Joey starts jogging backward, toward the street. "All right," he calls when he's not too far off. "Follow the ball with your eyes." He makes a pitch, and the neon goes up, but not so high. It comes down, close, close, close, and I reach for it. I feel the hairy sting of the rubber against my hands. I hear it bounce the ground. From inside the house, I hear Harvey going at it, scratching his nails against the window. I turn and see him staring wildly at us.

"You nearly had it," Joey says.

"Try again?"

"Throw it back." He shows me how to lift my elbow up and bend my wrist. How to give the thing a thrust. It goes up high, toward the crooked limbs of the tree. It comes down near, going practically no distance.

"You throw like a girl," Joey says, and laughs.

"Guess I do."

"You can get better." He picks up the ball and tosses it my way, underhand. This time I catch it. It stings. I smile.

Joey jogs backward and stops. "Send me a slider," he says. I throw my hardest. The ball slams down into the ground and takes off in a high bounce. Joey tucks his chin in and pumps his elbows, runs fast. He turns and lobs the ball back to where I'm standing. It bounces. I chase it. I turn and toss. The ball bounces worse than the others.

"What's a slider?" I ask.

"Not *that*." Joey laughs. "Not even close." He tosses the ball and I catch it.

From inside the house, I hear Harvey going crazy—scratching his long nails against the windowpane, whining and growling and crying. Joey stops and takes a long look in his direction, tries talking Harvey down, but Harvey won't listen. After a while Joey turns back to me and says that he's sorry. "Aunt Helen," he says, "has kind of been sick. I gotta go."

"That's okay."

"Come back?"

"Maybe tomorrow."

"I'll come for you," he says. "Right?" And I say, "No. I'll come for you." Fast and urgent I say it, my heart pounding hard. "Please," I say, and Joey takes a half step back and makes a long, thoughtful tug at a freckle.

"All right," he says.

"All right?" I say. "You promise?"

"You come for me. That's how you want it."

"Thanks," I say.

"For what?"

"For teaching me to play."

"That's kind of nothing," he says. "Wait until you learn the slider."

"You better go," I say, pointing to the steamed-up,

scratched-up window, to the house beyond the garden. I'd like a garden like that. I'd like a house with that rainbow for a porch. I'd like to go inside, where Joey lives, and forget the icosahedron.

"Harvey wouldn't have hurt you," Joey says, walking backward now, toward his house. "Just so you know, he wouldn't have."

"How do you know?"

"My friends are his friends. Rules, if you're my dog."

"Good rules," I say, and I feel my face go flushed.

"Don't forget," he says, "about tomorrow."

"Tomorrow."

Emmy

❧   ❧   ❧   ❧

The baby is missing. The baby is not where I left her—checked the rope and strapped her in, pulled my weight into the branch above, and said out loud, "This is good and nice and sturdy." I nudged her high and sang to her, "*True, true, the sky is blue*," and she smelled like baby. There is not one single other thing that smells like baby, that cheeks against your cheek like the cheek of a baby. I kissed her. I promised, "I am coming right back, Baby."

There was a pluming plane overhead. Two white trails of smoke, and a second plane—smaller, chasing. I had wanted a blanket so that I might lie nearby, so that all afternoon it would be Baby in her swing and me on the spine of the earth below, watching the ants in their jungled green, waiting for the red-tailed hawks to slice the plumes from the planes. It is twenty-eight steps to the back door, which is red because I painted it red, and it is nine steps to the downstairs closet, but I'd forgotten: I'd left the blanket upstairs, in the trunk by the bed, beneath the hooked rug Mama was working when she passed, beneath Mama's collection of hats. There are thirteen steps up, and there are thirteen steps down, and when I opened the red door where the brushstrokes had dried rough around the brass plate, Baby was gone.

There was a yellow sock on the ground, below the swing— the color of a chick, Baby's best color. She was always kicking off her socks, my baby.

It hasn't rained for weeks. The earth is bone. There were no shoe prints in the grass, no signs. There were no cars in the street, and the woods behind the house are deep. I heard a crackle and I ran, and maybe it was squirrel scuttle on leaves, maybe it was the hooves of deer, but I kept going in the direction of the sound, through the ragged scrapes of early-autumn trees, my skirt poked and unthreaded by the hard tips of the low branches, until all I could hear was the weight of me and my baby's name in the shadows: "Baby! Baby!"

My baby is gone. My baby is gone, and I should have called the police first thing. I should have had a decent, right-thinking thought in my head instead of growing desperate in the trees, draining the day of precious daylight with my every failing footstep. Peter came home to the red circle of the law's lights, to the house torn inside out and bright with every watt we own. To dogs in the woods and yellow rivers of light. They told Peter right at the end of his second shift. He smells like refinery and trouble, like the smoke up and down the river.

"Where's Baby?" Peter asks me now, the skin around his nose flaring the way it gets before his eyes go stone-cold blue.

"She dropped her sock," I say.

"Where's Baby?" he says again, louder, and it takes Sergeant Pierce and another cop to keep Peter's paws off me. He'd throttle me if they'd let him. He'd throttle me like he's done before. "Let him do," I say. "Just. Please." Because I'm done, dead and gone, if I don't have Baby.

"What's the mother's first rule?" Peter says to the sergeant. "What is it? You know what it is."

The sergeant looks from Peter to me with sergeant eyes.

"Taking care," Peter answers himself. "Taking care is the first mother rule. I tell her every day: Take care. Every morning I leave here I say it. Every night when she tucks Baby into bed." His face is lit-up lava. The pupils in his eyes aren't stones but hurricanes.

"Mr. Rane, we have a situation. Step back, now, and lower your hands. If you love your baby like you say you do, you'll give us room to do our work."

Peter lowers his fists.

"Be useful," the sergeant says sternly. "Make me a list of the people you know. Anybody anywhere who could be out for a little revenge."

"Ask her," Peter says.

"Ask me what?" I say.

"Ask her what she was doing upstairs when my daughter was out back, all by herself, defenseless, in a swing. Ask her: Is that a mother?"

"We'll be looking," the sergeant says, "after every possible lead."

Sophie

I made the world's best icosahedron. Like my life depended on it, I made it. Arranged it pretty on the cutting board, put it front and very central, on the kitchen table. Like the flowers you see on the TV shows, that's how I displayed it. So that when my mother came home, it would be the first thing she saw—not me, in my changed clothes, feeling hopeful.

"Look," I said. "It turned out perfect."

"And did you learn," Mother asked me, "about the principles of solids?"

"Archimedean solids," I said. She stood, judging, not speaking. She held her head to the left, then to the right, and closed one eye and sighed.

"Here," she said. "Help me with this." She handed me the Styrofoam leftovers box that she had brought back from work. I popped the lid on a pair of hot dogs. "One for each," she said, and I put the dinner out. I offered her mustard and ketchup, waited for notes, a little discussion, but she said nothing, and I worried that she knew, or maybe guessed, that I'd been lazy. When she finished her hot dog, she stood and dragged herself away from the table. I stayed behind, thinking about Joey and sliders. I heard her climb to her room and shut the door. I made my way to the attic.

Which is where I am now, looking out at the night above and Joey's house below, the big tree between. There are yellow flames in his rectangle windows, curtains folding in with the breeze. I lean out as far as I can, get near as I can to Joey. I watch the windows, looking for signs of him look-ing for signs of me. I see the edge of a hallway, the back of a chair, the half of a table, and finally Harvey, rousing up the air around him, Aunt Cloris on his tail. When she sits at the slice of kitchen table I can see, she picks up a long knife and starts splitting envelopes. She writes out a list. Harvey settles. No Joey.

Up here, alone, I wonder how I could ever explain— how I got here, how long I'll stay here, how it has been. I'd have to start with Chap, the cat I lost. I'd have to go all the way back to the almost beginning, when Chap, my cat, disappeared. I was four. I was alone.

"Chap!" I cried. "Chap!" But I'd opened the door just to test the day, and he was through the yard and down the walk, wicking his tail all around. He zagged toward the street, then into the street and up the black asphalt road, where a long yellow bus with big fat wheels was coming too fast in his direction. "Chap!" I screamed, and then I was out there on the walk and in the street, hollering against the wind in the direction of the school bus. I heard the slamming squeal of the brakes on the bus. I saw Chap's fluffy tail beneath the hulking yellow. I kept running until the bus had stopped, and then I didn't see Chap, and then I lost him.

"You be careful," I heard the bus driver call—an angry voice, a reprimand, the kids behind him laughing. But his anger was like nothing compared to my mother coming home—my mother finding the door unlocked, Chap gone. "I told you" is what she said. "I told you about doors. About safety." I was four and it was all my fault. We found a better house, with better locks. We kept on moving. "It's you and me now," my mother always said, and every single time, she meant it.

Emmy

"I told you that we shouldn't have done," Peter says.

"Done what, Peter?" I'm shaking. I want him to hold me, but he'd never. I want him to tell me we'll find Baby. But there is hardly a difference in his mind between me and the crime that's been committed, and the rains have come in, and the dogs have quit searching; they'll start again tomorrow. "We'll be looking after every possible lead," the sergeant said. Peter's hurricane eyes storm through me. He wells up inside himself and turns away.

"Shouldn't have done had Baby."

"You don't want Baby?"

"I don't want *this*. You were her mother."

"*Were*, Peter? She's not a *were*."

I can't keep my heart in my chest. I can't breathe, and I can't stop walking back and forth, back and forth, the north and south of nowhere. Peter stands at the window, looking out into the night, big as he has ever been. He wasn't big like that when I met him in high school. He bullied himself up since with a pair of dumbbells, a glass of egg yolk and milk with his morning coffee. "What are you training for?" I used to ask him. "The Olympics?"

"I married you for your cheesecake," he used to say. My mama's recipe, passed on. Mama taught me every kitchen thing I know. Peter fell in love with my cooking.

"Somebody took her," he says now. "What does somebody want with our Baby?"

I can't abide; I can't. I think of Baby in her swing, way up high and smiling. I think of me, finding Baby, never losing Baby, always near my Baby. It's eight steps to the stairs and thirteen steps up. I pull my canvas Keds from the closet shelf. I dig the purse that Mama left me out from the bottom of the trunk. I trade my cotton skirt for my roll-up Levis. I stick a comb in my back pocket. There are thirteen steps down, and the front door is white. I'm out in the night, searching for Baby.

"Emmy Rane!" I hear Peter bark after me. "Emmy Rane, where do you think you're going?" But I won't come home until I have her back. I won't.

It has kept on with the rain—big fat drops that taste like dew. All these weeks without rain, and now it comes, but from only half the sky; the other half has half a moon hanging huge, and I follow the moon, straight-ahead west, and now south and now again west, at the bend in the road. Baby's eyes are round; they are living sapphires. She will not close them, I am sure, until she sees me coming.

Baby, I am coming.

My Keds make *whisper hurry hurry* sounds across the

cement walk. In the broken places, in the cracks, it's getting sloppy. I feel a dampness sinking in around my toes and wish I'd remembered socks, but I'm not going back and it isn't cold, just a little chilly beneath the eye of the moon. They searched the whole woods—the police and their dogs. They went partway up the railroad tracks on the opposite side of the trees, until, with the dark and the rain, they called for quitting and asked for more photos, said they would call out all the forces. I don't know where they'll go tomorrow, what leads they think they have, who they imagine would do this, or why, what time they'll drink their coffee and start. But I can't wait. I won't. The moon is my lamp, and I follow. My heart is a sick, soft place, and my lungs are very small.

On the street, the houses are all lit up like jack-o'-lanterns or blued through with TV. "We're not getting any TV," Peter says. I asked him only once. Sometimes I wish I'd married Kevin O back when I had choices. There was a row of daffodils behind his mother's house, and in spring he'd cut me some. But Peter was three years older than me, and he had a job already, working at the refinery. He had the '82 Nissan pickup that he said someday he might teach me how to drive. "When you're ready," he said. "I'm ready," I told him. "When I say you're ready," he said.

I wish I were driving now. I wish I had wheels and speed, a map that would take me right this instant to my baby. The night is knots and splash, drips and skid, and one road has ended and another begins, and the lone whistle of a long train roars by. The neighborhood changes—from houses to retail, from window light and TV flicker to lanterns up above. At the gas station, the pumps are still. At the Clock and Watch, the gutter is splash. Maybe they're hiding Baby in the shadows between places, in the dark behind bushes, on the other side of barrel trash cans. Maybe she's there, in the back room of Reilly's Saloon. Baby's head makes a snug fit inside my palm. She taught herself smiling. She's a genius at smiling. If she's out here, near, I will find her.

A car goes by, soaking me through. My feet are two pale fish inside the tight ponds of my Keds. I leave the street for the train station. I leave the station and cross onto the tracks, slick-backed and shiny as snail glisten. The black gauze of the clouds flap at the moon, and from the tracks I can see into the backs of people's houses, the private places where the lamps have not gone off. It's like looking through snow globes, worlds behind glass. If Baby were there, in any of those houses, I would see. But all I see is that tower of folded towels and that face of a cat and that woman slipping a nightgown down over her shoulders. All I see is a man in a burnt-orange chair, reading the newspaper, wearing his glasses on the bald glow of his head.

No one rocking Baby. No one cooing at Baby. No one holding her up to the night.

The sop inside my Keds is growing chill. My jeans have

worked themselves loose at the waist. The air smells like skunk and peroxide. Before Baby was born, that's what bothered Peter most—that I smelled things he said weren't there.

"You're just imagining," he'd tell me.

I'd tell him, "Am not." My way of smelling, it runs in the family. My way of seeing, too, my way of explaining: it was Mama's before mine, and it now belongs to Baby.

"Baby!" I call into the night. "Baby!"

But my voice skids away, rides the slippery tracks. Far away, at the bend in the rails, the night is lamped. It is yellow and growing brighter, and now I understand: the train has big yellow eyes. Lovely ocher liquid eyes. They put the shimmer down on the tracks and splatter the dark. Now the train is past the bend. Now it throws its wide eyesight into the lean between things. The ballast and sleepers start to rumble at my feet. The rails clink up and down, and the longer I stand here, the louder they clink, like some soprano heart. *Be smart*, I tell myself. *Be calm.* I turn and stare into the night. If Baby can't be found, I do not wish to be found either.

Rumble and clink. Brighter and loud. The fish of my feet in the sloshing puddles. *Train, come and get me. Take me to Baby. Find me my one little girl.*

And then "Jesus Christ," a voice says. "Jesus Christ, what were you thinking?"

His weight is a monster bat fallen from the sky. Through

the rumble of lamplight, I am dragged. Across the brightening rails, I am banged, bones against steel against steel.

"Leave me alone," I tell the monster. "Leave me be." But I can't wrestle free and I can't stand, can't feel my own weight in the hard wind of the train passing, can't touch the steely cars, because my arms are knotted up with his and my ankle is a crack of pain and he is stronger and insisting.

"Out on the tracks with a train coming? Are you crazy?" He has a brogue in his voice. He is loaded down with gravity, dragging me now past the final ballast scatter to the tall grass margin along the track, and staying low while the train roars by. Chains and speed. Unzipping light. Me wrenching and yanking, unfree.

"I'll call the police," I say. "I'll have them arrest you." Calling the words out over the train roar. His weight is a shackle.

"You were standing on the tracks."

"I know where I was."

"The train was coming."

"I was looking for something. For someone." The train is high. The train is speed. The final car sears past, and that is when, at last, he loosens his hold—not altogether, but enough so that I might breathe. My leg is a long, lean pole of pain. "You broke my ankle," I tell him.

"You'd have been killed."

"It doesn't matter," I sob. "I lost my Baby." They are weather words, thick suds of sorrow. "She was stolen." All this time I have not seen the man's face. To someone looking down on us, we might seem one body, two heads.

"What's her name?" he asks at last.

"Baby," I sniff, and saying her name hurts me more than I can bear.

"Baby?"

"Only four months old," I say.

He says nothing for a good long time. My ankle hurts, my heart hurts, like everything is broken. I'm inside out with the leftovers of rain. "You've told the police?" he asks at last.

"Of course."

"Then let them do their work and find her. Go home. Wait for them there."

The tall grass is a wet itch up to my hips. My ankle is a church dome, a balloon. "I can't," I say. "Peter hates me. Peter blames me. I am his suspect number one."

I cannot stand on one leg, I cannot run. There is a man in a crouch behind me with a brogue in his voice, and in the dim light, I lean back and crank my head to get a dark, blurred look at him. His forehead is big and hangs low on his face. His eyes are tucked into caverns. His nose is a tulip bulb laid on its side. His mouth is too small for his face.

"What are you doing out here?" I ask him.

"The trains," he says after a long time. "I like to watch them."

Up above, the gauze clouds are still flapping at the moon. Down the tracks, the train vanishes. Across the way, one by one, the lamps go out in the houses. The alleys are dark. A trash can rattles. Baby could be anywhere, or she could be nowhere, too. I have no time, and no direction, and no faith in Sergeant Pierce.

"Baby is lost," I say at last, and I think he understands me, this man, because he doesn't move, and he doesn't hurt me, and he doesn't say, *Stop crying. There, there, we'll fix it.* He smells like garlic and chicken bones.

"Maybe it isn't broken," I say after a lot more time goes by. I test my ankle to prove my theory, squish my Keds to the ground. But the pain goes right up my pole leg, and I cry out.

"It wasn't hurting you that I was after," he says.

"I know."

"I was just here, watching the train, and there you were. You had your back to it. I thought you couldn't hear it."

I can bend my ankle, but it hurts bad. I can move my foot an inch to the left, an inch to the right, but the swollen dome of my ankle scrapes the cotton ridge of my Keds. "I can't go home," I say, "until I find Baby."

"That was the last train of the night," he says.

"Tell me what to do," I say. "Tell me where to find her."

"I don't know how people think. People who steal babies. I don't know where they hide."

"I have Baby's sock," I say. "Yellow." I reach for my purse

and I dig inside. "Baby didn't like her socks," I say. "She dropped them all around."

"Sounds like any other kid," he says.

"She wasn't any other."

"You want to tell me about her, then? Would it help any?"

"The only thing that would help would be finding her," I say.

"You want to tell me anyway?"

"Maybe," I say. "I don't know."

"It's your choice."

I let the darkness fall between us. I let the silence go on and I let the tears come up and I let the stars that come out shine and then there's nothing for me but talking—telling this strange, dark man how the happiest of all my days was the day Baby was born. "As though I was born right alongside my little girl," I say, and he nods—I think he does. I tell him how Mama died before she made acquaintance with my Baby, and how I've learned mothering on my own and also from the doctor who wrote the book of rules that tells you what to do. I married the same week I graduated high school, I say, and then I explain as how by then I didn't have choices, and I've done all of my new learning on my own.

"She chews the tip of her fourth finger," I say. "She'll fix her eyes on pretty things. She likes daddy longlegs and a finch on a tree and the puppet I sewed out of one of Peter's socks. She liked the day I took her into the woods behind our house. She liked the finch we found—pretty and yellow."

"I like birds," the man says.

"Nobody knows when Baby needs what she needs, except for me," I say, and now I'm crying again. I cannot stop.

"The world's not right," he says, and his big hands squeeze the place on my arm just past the knob of my shoulder. He's a big man, and he's awkward.

Sophie

❄   ❄   ❄   ❄

In her La-Z-Boy throne she sits—her feet bony bare on the foldout stool, a Ziploc of ice on each knee, her hair splitting at her shoulders but not falling straight, not curling nice, only bunching and sagging over her faded work shirt. To her side, the sun pushes against the tight velvet curtains. Behind, the stairs go up, break a landing, turn their way up some more. Beside her is the table of library books in their shiny, noisy sleeves.

"'Although many solid figures having all kinds of surfaces can be conceived, those which appear to be regularly formed are most deserving of attention,'" she reads, from a book by a guy called Pappus. "'Those include not only the five figures found in the godlike Plato, that is, the tetrahedron and the cube, the octahedron and the dodecahedron, and fifthly the icosahedron, but also the solids, thirteen in number, which were discovered by Archimedes and are contained by equilateral and equiangular, but not similar, polygons.'" Her glasses have slid to the end of her nose, leaving little red marks on the bridge. The long hairs of her eyebrows make a sad tangle with her lashes. Something about the Archimedeans makes my mother lonesome, but there's no guessing at what. All I know is that it's Sunday morning and a boy lives next door, and I am itching to see him, and that my mother's giving a lesson on the Archimedeans instead, because my icosahedron wasn't perfect.

"Mother," I say, "shouldn't you be resting? With work and all, and your knees?"

"Be grateful," she says. "Pay attention."

I open my mind to the great outside—to the sun way past and the stirring of wings. I hear my mother starting in on the thirteen glorious solids: The truncated tetrahedron. The cuboctahedron. The truncated octahedron. The rhombicuboctahedron. The icosidodecahedron. Words like the parts of a song in a language I don't speak. Birdsong, maybe, or wing tune. "'Figures of thirty-two bases,'" she's saying. "'Twenty triangles and twelve pentagons.'" She leans back and the La-Z-Boy squeaks the way it has always squeaked since she found it along the side of some curb. "Looks like a turtle," I told her when she brought it home. "It was lost," she said, "and now it's found."

"You hear that?" I ask Mother now.

"Hear what?"

"The birds outside."

She pulls the glasses from the end of her nose and stares at me with her hard black eyes. "What did I tell you?" she says.

"To pay attention," I answer.

"To me," she says. "Not to the birds."

I uncross my legs. I cross them. I snake the one around the other and pull both together tight until they hurt bad and my legs go numb and I uncross them and unbend them and unsnake them and then curl up into a ball to rub the blood back into my leg. My mother waits for me to finish, then reads again, all glory to the snub dodecahedron. "'Ninety-two bases,'" she says. "'Eighty triangles and twelve pentagons.'" As if she designed the thing herself.

"That's nice," I say. "Real nice." Adding the *real* for effect.

She trades the one book in her lap for another from the tower and starts flipping through with her long, long hands until she finds a picture of the snub dodecahedron, which somebody built out of snips of bright paper. The snub dodecahedron puts my icosahedron to shame, which is, I know, my mother's point.

"See what is possible," she says.

"Um-hmmm."

"See how lovely they are, the Archimedean solids?"

"Seems kind of abstract," I say. "If you're asking me."

"Why am I," she groans, "the only one taking an active interest in your future?"

Active interest in my future? I think. But I've got plenty of that. I'm interested in Joey next door. In his teacup aunt and his stick-skinny aunt. In his big dog, a friend of mine, if I'm a friend of Joey's. In learning to throw better than girls are meant to throw.

"It's very nice," I say, hoping to ease her.

"What is?"

"Your snub dodecahedron."

She studies me, can't decide if I am lying.

"We have Sir Johannes Kepler to thank," she finally continues, "for rediscovering Pappus's notes on the Archimedean solids and sharing his knowledge with others. Pappus lived in the fourth century AD and Kepler thirteen centuries later. Sometimes history is in the hands of one man, or even in the hands of a woman." She closes the book and her eyes. My mother, I realize, is lonesome for Kepler, for the man with Archimedes's history in his hands.

"I'm sorry," I tell her. "For not paying better attention."

"You'll write an essay," she says, "to make things right. Five pages on the travels and lives of the truncated icosahedron. There's plenty here," she says, sweeping her hand toward the books, "to get you started."

"The travels and lives?"

"You heard me."

"A whole essay?"

"How is that so hard?"

"But, Mother . . ."

"Nothing more."

She lifts her knees, and the ice packs fall. She levers the foldout stool back into the La-Z-Boy's mouth and pushes up and groans. She hands me the book of photographs, then hobble-hops toward the stairs. "Seek perfection," she says, "in all that you do."

Perfection, I want to say, because look where we live, look where we are—in a house with a tumbledown roof and cracks in the floors and walls so full of old picture holes you'd think somebody had gone off shooting bullets. "What's the point?" I ask instead.

"The point of what?"

"Of learning Archimedean solids?"

"If you were a smarter girl, you wouldn't have to ask."

"I thought you said—"

"I'm going to bed."

"*Mother.*"

"The clock is ticking," she says, scraping her way up the stairs, her ice already puddling the floor.

The next morning, she walks the path, creaks open the door to the old Volvo, turns the motor over. I run. Up the stairs and into the attic, over the crossbeams and the pink fluff, toward the window. Outside, the sun is pale and liquid. The crows are big and black. They knock their way around the sky, then knock back down into the crooked tree. Flying and settling and returning and flying, and now the biggest crow caws down from the wide green crown and looks through the window at me.

I throw the sash up, push my head out, and watch as the sergeant crow stares and blinks, hops branches and twigs, hunches up his rubbery wings. When the door to Joey's house swings open, the sergeant flies and the other crows fly, and now when I look past the tree, I see Miss Cloris standing at the edge of her porch, wearing a rainbow-striped tee and a bow in her hair. She lifts her glasses from the string around her neck and fits them to her nose and stares up at the tree, as if she's wondering if the crows were a dream. She stares for a good long time, then shakes her head. "Now, that was a bona fide crow party," I hear her say to Harvey, who has scratched in beside her and held himself to the ledge of the rainbow-striped porch, looking like he'll fly, too, any second. She hums a little something, puts her hand on Harvey's head. He wags his tail stupendously. "You bad old pup," she tells him, and now when she looks up into the crazy branches of the tree, she stops and shades her eyes with her hand.

"Hey," she calls. "You growing an aviary over there?"

I shrug, don't answer.

"You know what an aviary is?"

"Not really."

"It's like a garden of birds. Takes a special someone to grow one."

She pulls the glasses from her nose and fixes the bow

right in her hair, crosses her arms across her chest, and waits for me to have something to say, but all of a sudden, I don't. "Pleased to meet you," she says at last. "My name's Miss Cloris. By the way."

"Sophie," I tell her.

"You Joey's friend?"

I nod. "He's teaching me to throw."

"Is he?"

I nod again. "He home?"

"Lucky for you," she says. "It's a teacher in-service."

"That's nice," I say, no idea just what she means.

"I take it you're waiting on Joey?"

"Maybe I am."

"Well, he's home, like I said. He's inside, with Miss Helen, reading her Cather. You know Willa Cather?"

I shake my head no.

"You an interrupter? When people read, you listen?"

"I like stories," I say.

"I like girls who like stories."

"I've been reading," I boast, "since I was three."

"And you never heard of Cather? *My Ántonia? The Song of the Lark? O Pioneers!?*"

"No."

"You best get yourself a Cather education. A girl can't live without Cather." She pauses. "You like to come hear Joey read? He does a nice Cather."

"Right now, ma'am?"

"Right now if you can swing it."

I stare down at her.

She stares up at me.

Harvey wags his tail, ferocious.

Mother finds out, and she'll kill me. Mother suspects, and we'll be gone, moving again and losing and dying, a little blacker every day, a little less something to fight for—and still, yet: the diner is that way, down the road, and my heart is pounding loud, and pounding louder.

"I'll stir up some lemonade on the off chance," Miss Cloris calls now. "Slice up some wedges of orange." She tugs at the bow in her hair and heads back toward the house. Harvey wallops his big tail behind her.

Emmy

I wait all night for the light of day, which will come laid flat out on the back of a train, Arlen, the big man, says. "You wait," he tells me. "You see." I am going nowhere in this soggy dark with this pole of pain for a leg; I'm waiting. I put my hand against the tender swell. It hurts something like a bee sting.

"Someone should take a look at that ankle," Arlen says.

"I've got bigger worries."

He has taken off his jacket and given it to me, laid it across my knees like a blanket. He has kept his arm across my shoulder, and I don't mind him, not really. I don't mind how he gives me room to tell my Baby stories, how he lets things be—no questions. I keep her just this close, all night long, with words and stories, the little songs that sometimes I will sing her. *True, true, the sky is blue.* I count down the minutes until dawn, when I can search again, when I will find her.

At last the day's first train crests the bend. "Just like I promised," Arlen says.

"You wait and watch for it every day?"

"I find it peaceful."

I watch in silence. I watch the ocher eyes swoosh the dark off the rails ahead, put their gloss of snail shimmer down. I feel the rattle in the hill where we sit, the air sucking crazy. Through the window in the booth above the pair of train eyes, I see the engineer and his straight-ahead face. I see the dangle of a light above his head.

"The first train is the express train," Arlen declares. "I like its speed."

The train screams and pitches. It thunders—such an awful trembling that I do not know how the houses on the banks along the tracks don't shatter up and crumble. My ankle swells in the raging roar. The jacket kicks up in a riffle from my knees until I press it flat with my hands.

"Watch it, now," he says, and he lifts his arm from my shoulder and rises up onto his haunches and balances here beside me in a way I wouldn't have thought he could. He's got something he knows about the miracle of the day's first train, and beside him I bear witness.

"Watch the ridgeline," he tells me, his voice drowning in the bellows of the train shooting past. When I look up to where he's pointing, I see a streak of tangerine touched down upon the silver-bodied train. Right there, like a horizon line, just as he has promised.

"Daybreak!" he hollers, and now he stands and pumps his fist to the sky, and the long strands of his graying hair get pulled about in the air suck. Finally the wind roars down, and the night has become a veil of shadows. The night isn't night, after all; it is first dawn.

Fast as it came, it leaves. When it's gone, Arlen squats back down beside me. His legs are wide but not long. His trousers are scruffy. He's missing a button on his blue-plaid shirt; there's a toothpaste stain on his collar. With the rising of the sun, he has been revealed. I am surprised by the pleasant way he smiles.

"Thank you," he says.

And I say, "What for?"

"For the company."

"That's funny," I tell him. "Funny sweet." *Like something Kevin O would say*, I think, *if Kevin O were in love with trains.*

Arlen rubs at his eyes with the fists of his hands. He looks a little cold without his jacket.

"Here," I say, lifting the jacket from my knees.

"Absolutely not," he says. "I'm the one who hurt your ankle."

"Saved my life is more like it."

"Well," he says, "you were standing there."

He isn't a pretty man or a handsome one. The bulb of his nose sits crooked. There's nothing on his outside that's as nice as his inside, but still. "Will you help me find my Baby?" I ask.

"Is there a plan?" he asks.

"I'm thinking."

"Can you stand on it?" he asks, and I say, "I don't much know if I can, but I know I have to."

He says, "Put it down slow," and now he takes the rise of the hill on his own, straightening his trousers all the way to his ankles, which, I see, in this breaking light, are naked. His shoes are the color of dried hay. His trousers are patched. His hands aren't like the rest of him, by which I mean, they are trim and the right size for hands. "Here," he says, as if he's inviting me to dance, and I put both my hands into his so he can give me the strength to stand, but when I try to ease onto my weight, it's like I've been hot-spiked.

"Oh, Arlen," I say.

He says, "Steady, now. I've got you."

"How am I going to find her," I ask, "if I can't walk?"

"Let's get you off the embankment," he says, "for starters. Incline can't be good for a gimpy ankle." I start hopping soon as he comes toward me. He takes my lean against his shoulder. His jacket has fallen to a pile on the ground. He makes sure I am steady before he bends down to retrieve it. I waver. When he again stands tall, I lean back in.

"You still feel a chill?" he asks.

"Sun is doing its job."

"You still working on your plan?"

"I don't have a plan."

"Then we need you home now. Soon as can be."

"Arlen, I told you. I said it already. I'm not going home without my Baby."

"Police will come knocking, and what will they do when

they find that you're gone? What will they think? What about your husband? They'll put you down on the suspects list, maybe. Jigger up some kind of motive. Mother on the lam, they'll say. If you don't have a plan, you risk suspicion."

"I would not hurt Baby."

"I know, but the police don't."

"You know about police, Arlen?"

"Maybe once or twice."

"What do you mean?"

He doesn't answer for a minute, longer. His hold grows tight on me, and anxious. "Doesn't matter," he says at last, and I don't come back at him with questions, because he still smells like chicken bones and garlic, still takes my weight like a Roman column. I don't mind, I decide it right now, whatever he's done. Arlen's to be trusted.

"Arlen?"

"What?"

"Where do you think they took my Baby?"

"Can't figure it."

"Who would have done it?"

"Jealousy," he says. "Or greed."

"I said *who*, Arlen."

He steps and I step and I let the ankle hang between us. He steps and he says, "Press your arm hard down on my shoulder—make it easier." I try what he says, but it's still not easy.

"I'm going to wear you out," I say, out of breath. We're up the incline and down now, in a gully. We're in a patch of grass that grows tall as my hips. Beyond the fog is the back portion of a modest garden shop. Piles of mulch and piles of earth. Pot after pot of bush and zinnia. I smell the steam of things growing. "Would like to steal us one of those wheelbarrows."

"Stealing's no good," Arlen says. "It's trouble."

"We'd bring it back," I say, "when we were done. Then it'd be lawful."

"It would still be trouble." When he talks now, he's wheezing. When he walks, he slants. I hop and he pulls and we drag, and now Arlen stops to collect himself. I stand beside him in the scratch of grass, my right arm sore from pressing hard across his back.

The sky is pinking. It is floating down onto the garden shop, peeking in through the greenhouse windows, putting a glance of gold onto the hump of mulch. It showers sun on the street beyond, where a few cars are already out trolling, their headlights streaking. I smell a lit cigarette. It burns through one of the shadows.

"Gardeners," Arlen says, guessing my question. "They start early."

"What time do you suppose it is?"

"Easing up on six, I'd wager."

I think of Peter at home, alone in our bed, or up on his feet. I think of what he will say when he sees me, what he must feel inside, if it's like what I feel inside. I guess I've always been afraid of Peter. From our first night alone, I have been, and now I know I cannot face him.

"How are you at holding on?" Arlen asks.

"Good enough," I say, "till yesterday." I sob and I can't help it.

"How are you at waiting?"

"Why are you asking?"

"I have a bike," he says. "A real sore loser of a bike, but it's something. You could ride the handlebars. It would be faster."

"You would do that, Arlen? Go home and then come back and get me?"

"I wouldn't leave you here," he says, "if that's what you're asking."

Sophie

"Oh, hon, sweetie, you came," Miss Cloris says, and when she lets me in to the front sitting room, it's as if I'm walking into Easter, all purple and green with a long white leather couch stuck up against one wall that turns and keeps going against the next wall, like an eggshell that's cracked. There are books on the floor and books on the sills, a cat lying low on a long, low table. I hear Harvey's nails clicking against the floor. When I turn, he leaps and pushes at my shoulders. His raw, wet tongue scrapes my skin.

"You behave, you bad old pup," Miss Cloris says, grabbing the dog by his collar and dragging him up the wall of steps, then past the eggshell couch, and shutting a door behind her. She returns, her toes pointing to either side as she walks. When she stands, she hardly comes up to my chin. "Puppy love," she says, scatting the dog hair off her shirt and fixing her hair bow. Now she takes me on a tour—past the kitchen, which is black, white, and yellow, past the bathroom, which is orange and red, and to the end of the house, which is sky blue and the color of new French fries. The sofas in this room are half the size of any sofa my mother has ever pulled in from the street—more like chairs wide enough to fit two people—and in one of those chairs sits the skinny one and Joey.

"Hey," he says when he sees me.

"Hey." I feel myself going hot, my heart going to flutters.

"Sophie Marks," Miss Cloris says, "meet my friend Miss Helen. Found Sophie in her window and invited her in. Claims she's not an interrupter."

"That so?" Joey says, and I feel myself going hotter as Joey looks me up and down with that crooked smile on his face and Miss Helen stares at me with eyes so blue I think they're green. Beside the stuffy chair, her wheelchair leans. Beyond the chair and Miss Helen, through a window screen, sits a strange silver thing, like a house on wheels that got stuck on the side of a road. It's shiny as the bottom of a new pan. It has white twinkle lights hung around its rim. The lights are on, though it's the middle of daytime. It looks rooted, like a tree.

"For when we take our cross-country," Miss Cloris says when she sees what I am staring at, and I nod, not knowing what she means. I look back into the room, where the blue-sky walls are stenciled over with French fry–colored words.

"Our favorite authors," Miss Cloris explains, as if she's following every movement of my eyes. "Their very best words. We paint them here so we don't forget them."

"You know Willa?" Miss Helen asks me. Her voice is small, almost a whisper.

"She will soon," Miss Cloris says.

"I know Kipling," I say. "I know Alcott."

"Well," Miss Helen says, "that's a good-enough start." Miss Cloris excuses herself and walks funny-toed to the kitchen. She returns with a tray of lemonades. "The party begins," she says, giving one tall glass to each of us, and now she tells Joey to read from where he stopped off. She squats into the second stuffy chair, pulling me down with her. Her end of the cushion sinks fast; mine goes higher. Joey takes a swallow of his lemonade, then smashes his cap down harder and rubs an itch off his nose, his lips twisted up in a funny smile. Harvey whines from his locked room upstairs. Everything else is silent.

"'Every conical hill was spotted with smaller cones of juniper, a uniform yellowish green, as the hills were a uniform red,'" Joey reads. "'The hills thrust out of the ground so thickly that they seemed to be pushing each other, elbowing each other aside, tipping each other over.'"

"We're in New Mexico," Miss Helen whispers. "1851."

"Death Comes for the Archbishop," Miss Cloris says, trying to whisper, too, but it comes out strange. "Cather's masterwork."

I look from one to the other. They both blink. Sit there as if they're expecting something smart to come from me, but I don't know Cather and I've never been to New Mexico and this is 2004, and besides, I have sworn up and down that I am not an interrupter.

"We like going on adventures," Miss Helen finally says. "Cather takes us along."

"By way of Joey, our reader," Miss Cloris says.

"Should I keep going, then?" Joey asks, and Miss Helen and Miss Cloris nod, like they're the same person with the same mind, except they couldn't be more different. Miss Cloris's hair is as puffed up wild as the bow that's stuck inside. Miss Helen's is long and white and soft. I look from one to the other, and Joey reads, and I'm not really listening at first. I'm thinking how strange it is to be sitting here, in another's house, and how the clock is ticking, and how the essay waits, and how my mother will kill me if she finds out, and how sweet and chill is this lemonade. *She will kill me. But then,* I think, *I can always outrun my mother.*

"'Under his buckskin riding-coat he wore a black vest and the cravat and collar of a churchman,'" Joey reads. "'A young priest, at his devotions; and a priest in a thousand, one knew at a glance. His bowed head was not that of an ordinary man,—it was built for the seat of a fine intelligence.'"

"One of literature's finest creations," Miss Cloris sighs, and just now, from down the hall, slinks the cat with its thick, silver-gray hair and its eyes blue-green as Miss

Helen's. Quiet, the big cat leaps and settles into the space between Miss Cloris and me, and Miss Cloris fits her hand to the cat's head without saying a word. The cat's heart hums, but the cat doesn't speak. Joey reads on, and that's all there is, except for my own heart, still beating.

Emmy

He comes not by the rails, but by the road—up the rubble of the nursery's drive, unsteady on the turf. His gray hair is blowsy in the breeze. Streamers ripple from his handlebar's cuffs. It's a girl's bike he has, with the fattest rubber wheels. Its seat is long and sparkly. The man at the nursery turns when Arlen rides by. He slips the cigarette out from between his lips and blows a smoke puff to the sky.

The ground rattles beneath my feet. "Train coming," Arlen says. He skids to a stop and dismounts, knocks the kickstand down. He walks the little distance through the forest of tall grass and reaches for my hands, and right when he does, a train roars by, just as he promised.

"Where are we going?" he asks, watching the train disappear.

"Straight to the big station," I tell him.

"That's the plan?"

I nod. "That's the plan, Arlen. Our first stop."

"You won't go home?" he asks again.

"No, I won't," I say.

He looks at me for a while without speaking. "We're talking about some distance."

The smoker keeps his eyes on us. Arlen gives me a tug, and I'm up. The slightest pressure and my ankle flashes fire. It's hurting worse than it did in the night, but I don't say it, because Arlen is feeling bad enough. I hop-walk to the bike with Arlen's help, then he turns me around and lifts me up. Fits me onto the bike's handlebar. Shows me where to wrap my fists. He steadies me; he steadies the bike.

"Back roads or direct roads?" Arlen asks when I'm fit, fixed and sure, into the handlebar's curve. The kickstand is up; Arlen's behind me.

"Fast as we can get there," I say.

"You don't mind us getting seen?"

"We've already been seen." I nod across the distance to the gardener standing there. He blows another smoke puff high and salutes me, like a veteran.

"You're sure?"

"I am."

I feel Arlen putting everything he has against me— digging down into the pedals with his feet, steering the front wheel straight as he can steer it across the nursery driveway's rubble. I squeeze so hard with my fists that my elbows hurt. I shift this way and that to keep my balance. Neither of us talk—not Arlen, not me—because going forward is taking everything we've got. Finally we make it out onto the street. Arlen stops the forward motion, stands behind me, panting.

"We've got the toughest part out of the way," he says between hard, hoarse breaths.

"Arlen," I say, "it just occurred to me. Today's a workday and you're missing work. I'm going to get you in trouble."

"Taken care of that," he says, still barely breathing.

"Already?"

"I left a note for my supervisor. Family emergency, I told him."

I feel my face flushing pink and red. "You're a sweet man, Arlen," I tell him.

"Something I've been meaning to ask you," he says.

"Emmy," I say. "My name. That what you wanted?"

"I suppose."

I wish I could turn and see him, but that would throw our balance. I wish I could touch my hand to his in a way that would let him know I am grateful.

"Ready?" he asks after saying nothing for a spell, and I feel the bike budge and shift, cut and weave, until at last we find ourselves gliding smoothly. Arlen keeps to the sidewalk wherever he can. On the roads, he pedals straight down the margins. It's still early enough that the traffic is light, and only three cars so far have honked at us crazy.

"You're good at this," I tell him.

"Holding on is its own talent," he says.

It's miles to the big station; I know as much. We've maybe gone one mile, and this is not your simple and easy. I try not to think of the hurricane eyes inside of Peter, the hurricane wrath. If I find Baby, Peter will forgive me. If I find Baby, finding Baby will be all that matters.

"You okay up there?" Arlen calls to me.

"Just fine," I call back. The sun has come up like a squint on the horizon. Most everything we travel by is pink. The glass in the shops. The windshields on cars. The glint flecks in the sidewalks and on the streets. I haven't seen a cop drive by. I've seen no posters on the trees. No one and nothing but me and Arlen searching for Baby. We take a ninety-degree angle hard and wobble our way back to a glide. My elbows hurt more than my fingers.

"How about you? You okay?" I call over my shoulder.

"Time is of the essence," Arlen says.

There's breeze in my hair, in my heart. *Baby,* I think, *I'm coming for you*, because this is the logic best as I can calculate: whoever took her will disappear as quick as the first train out will take them. They wouldn't leave last night, when the police and their big-nosed dogs were hunting. But they'd leave right now, under dawn's smoky cover, when the police are still stirring into coffee.

"Arlen," I say, "you are my hero."

"Least I could do," he says, puffing.

Sophie

❖   ❖   ❖   ❖

"That's it?" my mother asks. "That's all you've written?"

She holds the single page as if it's a smelly onion peel, shakes it as if it's crumbs, knocks it down between her hamburger and the ketchup. Her name tilts on her uniform pocket. Her hair slips free from her bun. She had a misery day and I've worsened it plenty. "One page," she says, "and not a single mention of the buckyball."

I swallow the last of my chips and meet her eyes. I steal a look toward my essay, blooming grease spots.

"The buckyball, Sophie. The roundest round molecule, the most symmetrical large molecule of all." She closes her eyes and sinks her face into the bones of her hands, and when the next piece of her hair falls loose, she sighs. Suddenly I wish I could tell Mother about Joey and his aunts, about the cat and the dog, about Father Latour and the red hills of New Mexico, the clover fields, the cottonwoods, the acacia. *What, I asked, is acacia? Acacia,* Miss Cloris answered. *Some call them whistling thorns. Whistling thorns,* I would say to my mother. Why can't we talk about that?

The light of the real day is gone. The lamplight is harsh.

My mother's hands are blue blooded and thin and heavy with her chin, and in the silence I remember her years ago, on the floor of a lost house, beside me. She'd bought a long roll of waxed white paper and pots of finger paints and said, "We'll paint what we dream." There wasn't white in her hair. There wasn't night beneath her eyes. She'd unrolled the paper across the width of the floor, and all afternoon we painted dreams. Hers were blue like sky. Mine were yellow-pink, like sun. Afterward, for the whole next week, her fingers were the color of the purple inside shadows.

"Mother," I say now, "I'll make it up to you. I promise."

"How's that?" she moans, her words mashed behind her hands.

"Tomorrow. You'll see. I'll surprise you."

She lifts her eyes and squints against the lamplight. She straightens the name on her shirt. "I'm awfully tired," she says. "Awfully so." She puts her hands down flat and pushes herself up from the table. She wobbles a little, then stands.

"Getting late," she says.

"I'll clean up," I tell her.

"Do some reading," she tells me. "Take an interest."

It's a half-moon night. The clouds float low, skimming the rooftops, gauzing the street lamps, and down there, low, past the cradle of the tree, Miss Cloris and Miss Helen swing from the wooden porch chair that hangs from silver chains. The swing creak is an evening song, bigger than their talk, bigger than crow rustle, bigger even than the sound of my mother snoring, one floor below.

Perfection. Mother uses the word, but nothing ever is; it's a false-hope word, an illusion. It's sitting inside Joey's house like I have a right to be there, like I won't be erased from this neighborhood if Mother figures her way to the truth. I didn't write my long essay because I didn't give it proper time. I didn't give it time because I didn't want to. I wanted to stay with Joey and his aunts and the archbishop and the hills. I wanted to stay where the cat Minxy sleeps, where they slip orange slices in with the fresh-squeezed lemonade, where I'm not supposed to be.

"Hey," I hear, and when I look up, I see the shadows that Joey makes, hanging out into the dark from his second-floor window.

"Joey," I ask. "What are you doing?"

"Looking out," he whisper-shouts, putting his hands up to his face. He blows the words across the alley of the yard and up so nobody else can hear them. I can't see more than the blur of him, the flopped, funny wilderness of his uncapped hair.

"Me, too," I say. "I'm looking out."

"You see the moon?"

"Sliced right in half."

"You see the crows?"

"They're black as night."

We stay quiet for a while, let the night songs sing.

"Joey?"

"Yeah?"

"You like school?"

"It's okay enough."

"You ever hear of Archimedean solids?"

"Not much."

"I guess she's right, then."

"Who's that?"

"My mother."

"Right on what?"

"Homeschooling," I say, and nothing more, and the night floats by, and Joey goes nowhere. After a while, he's talking again.

"Bus comes round at seven o'clock," he says.

"Yeah. I've seen it."

"School's not so far down the road."

"That's nice."

"Funny things happen at school. You should take a ride, see the school from inside."

"Can't," I say. That's all. Because saying one thing will lead to another and another.

"You think you'll ever go to school?"

"Maybe someday."

"College?"

"College!"

"I'm aiming for college."

"Well, good for you, Joey," I say. "Good for you." The skin beneath my eyes gets tight.

"Sorry we didn't get around to the throwing lessons," Joey says after a while.

"I didn't mind."

"Miss Helen needed a story."

"I liked it fine."

"You coming back?"

"I probably might."

"You're not mad or anything?"

"Not mad."

"All right."

"Moon's going away. Getting higher."

"I'm guessing it's time."

"All right. Night, Joey."

"Night, Sophie."

"See you tomorrow?"

"I will."

Save the Cather for me, I want to say. *Save Harvey. Save Minxy.* And the moon is higher and his window goes hollow and I am left alone and lonesome. In most every house we've ever come to, the people who have lived ahead of us have left something behind. Maybe the kitchen table, for being too small, or the lamps, for being so ugly, or a painting, because it's a reminder of something it might be good to forget. We're takers, Mother and I, moving the left-behinds on—the birdcage nobody wanted, the picture frames that got abandoned, the painted dresser, the collection of knobs. "What will we do with the knobs?" I said. "They'll find their purpose," Mother told me. Renting is for people like us, Mother says. For collectors, for carrying forward.

The last people to live in this house left in a hurry. Left the stains still on the linoleum floor, the curtains still hanging, the shoe boxes toppled in the hallway closet. In the pantry they left cans of tomatoes, and rice. In the living room they left a torn-cushion rocker. They left drawings by little kids and a bag of blue marbles, a collection of dried ladybug wings, set out like beads. "We'll get to it," my mother said, but everything is still like it was—our things squeezed between their things, the library books in their tower, the boxes we carry from house to house stacked up in the closets or the basement.

"I'll make it up to you," I said. I promised, and I mean to, lying here on my borrowed bed, flipping through library pages on the genius of solids. It's Kepler I keep coming back to, Kepler, who makes me remember my mother's sighing smile, and the more I index back to Kepler, the more I'm sure: I will write my ode to him, which has to be better than writing five pages on an icosahedron—has to be. "From Nothing to Big Things" I'll call it, starting with Kepler's poor and sickly birth and heading straight through his laws of planetary motion, his honoring of the pinhole camera, his optics and the words he used to explain the moon and its pull on the tides. I can see, the more I read, why my mother was sighing over Kepler, his work on the Archimedean solids being pretty much the least of his greatness. "From Nothing to Big Things." I write the title in fancy script across the top of the page and then I sit here and think. It is dark down the hall and down the stairs. Dark straight up to the high half-moon. My mother snores like a train coming through.

Emmy

❦　　❦　　❦　　❦

Up a cut of curb, Arlen angles. Past the window streak of the old diner, beneath a sign for Kodachrome, down. We reach the west edge of the university, and Arlen pedals through— past the first of the early risers, a dog that doesn't mind us. The station lies east in a haze, beneath a fidget of shadows, and the streets grow wider than they were before, less still and undercover. Cars drive by, and people pass. An old man with a dog. A lady shaped like a stick. A pair of boys with a pack of cards. No Baby. The walk beneath us is broken, snagged. My ankle is a bowl of glass, and with every bump and bang, it shatters.

The smell of fumes is on us. There's a chemical sky. Behind me I hear the soft howl of air escaping Arlen's lungs, the push-through-and-forward of his knees, and now we have come to where we are, and we are still going. The pole of pain that was my leg is my arms now, too. It is my hands and fingers, which have hardened into twist and bone. Up ahead, I spy the local trains in their silver gleams, the white rise of the old station, cut as if from marble, the flower seller making her roses—poking the stems into buckets of water and flapping a blanket to the ground, adjusting a sign. Her roses are yellow; they are red.

One block more. Three quarters. One half. Arlen riding the curb cuts like a master. A taxi speeds to the curb and stops, and when the bright door pops apart and the two men get out, I know they are not the thieves of Baby. I know that the woman in the green dress leaning against the yellow-brick of station wall is, likewise, not hiding Baby, nor the man and the woman, cuddled close as they make their way near. I have Baby's sock in my purse. I have the smell of her in my heart. I have instinct, the mother's kind. I will know when I am near to Baby.

"Slowing her down," Arlen calls out from behind. "Brace yourself." And now we are hitching on the broken-up walk and jouncing hard and jittering near upon the crowd that's not so much gathered as converging at one of the station's many glass doors. I hear the squeal of the applied brake behind me and the big slap of Arlen's shoe on the ground. I hear the second shoe slapping down, and in the tumult and pitch of the almost stop, I cannot hold on. I am heaped upon the walk, smashed down, the front wheel of Arlen's bike riding the hill of my spine.

Arlen's on me in a second, his big bat-wingy arms. "Emmy," he says. "Emmy, I'm sorry."

Already a trickle of blood has opened high on my elbow and that old man's loose mutt is quick to my heels. "Get,"

I tell the dog, and Arlen smacks it on the rear. And then he puts his arms around me, big and tight. When the mutt starts barking, the old man says, "Come," and despite all of those who have stopped to stare, despite the shatter of my ankle, the rip-through near my elbow, no one reaches in with help, not one.

"I had to brake," Arlen says.

"Don't start with feeling bad. We made it is all."

I look beyond him to the station door, to the people coming early, the people from taxis. Everywhere is the smell of train metal and speed. I scan the outside crowd for lumpishness, wrong parcels, babies, but I know what's true: whoever has her is not here in this morning's sun. It's a dark thing this one has done; dark keeps to darkness. To the wooden benches lined up like church pews inside the station. To the cool blue corners near the sweet blued walls. On the other side of the sunbeams that the station lets in through its high panes of glass.

Arlen is careful with all the pieces of me. He lifts me upright off the ground, with my bad leg hanging. He tips the sleeve of his jacket toward the blood on my arm, but I put out my right hand to stop him.

"Don't you spoil that jacket of yours," I tell him. "You've done enough."

"Known you since last night," he says. "And look." Meaning my ankle. Meaning my arm.

"I won't hear such nonsense talking," I say. Because what matters now is what happens next. What matters is that we find my Baby before she's put on a train and taken to where I won't know enough to follow. The fender of Arlen's bike is smashed. Its streamers are all crinkled. It looks like a puddle down there on the walk, some other thing needing rescue.

Arlen smoothes his frizzled hair, tugs at his shirt. He pulls a chain and padlock from his trouser pocket and pulls out a key. "Wait for me," he says, hop-walking me to the stretch of wall where the lady in green stands, unmoving, a patch of warm on her face. I lean against the wall beside her, until I'm certain I won't fall. I watch Arlen scoop up the bike and weave it to a nearby barrel trash can. He strings some part of the chain through the bike's front wheel and loops the rest around the barrel, loops and loops it. He takes more time than I wish he would, but Arlen's very careful. All of a sudden, a white police car with its red blare on is speeding past and my thoughts speed with it—home to Peter and the empty swing, to the sergeant finally finished with his coffee. Gone to our house, maybe. Asking Peter, And your wife? Where is she?

"Where are you going?" the woman beside me asks, in a dreamy voice, as if I'm headed out on some vacation. As if I had not just been thrown from the handlebars of a bike and smashed to the walk far below. As if my left arm and right leg aren't practically broken—maybe broken. Her cheeks are rouged.

———

"Something's been stolen," I say. "Someone."

"Hmmm," she says, and never opens her eyes, and I think that maybe she's lost something, too, and I look to Arlen, across the way, wrapping the final loop of locking chain around his girl-style bike and patting the back of the trash can.

"Arlen," I call, "will you hurry up, please?"

"I am going away," the woman beside me murmurs. "My honeymoon. I'm just standing here, waiting for my honey."

Honeymoon, I think. Honeymoon. Honey.

I think of Peter at home, in his fury. I think of Sergeant Pierce asking, "And your wife?"

Sophie

❈   ❈   ❈   ❈

The bus roars around the corner, chokes up, shudders, then roars again, and Joey's gone. I heard his front door slam and his shoes skip the walk, heard Harvey going wild and Miss Cloris calling, "Go out and conquer, Joey Rudd." Now the day feels wrapped in plastic, and I am trapped on this side of here.

"I'm leaving," my mother had called up the stairs at the early-shift hour. "Be good."

"Planning on making it all up to you," I called back, but if she heard me, she didn't answer.

"From Nothing to Big Things"—that's all I've got: the title. All this night long, and that's it, my ode for Mother. "I've poured my whole life into you," she is given to reminding, and it's been a hard life, too, getting out from under the No Good, our reason for running. "Your mother knows best," she says when we are on the move again, on the chase or ahead of it, just in front of it. When I was small, I thought the No Good lived in the outsides of things—that night came on because of it, that badness was coming my way. But I have been safe, all thanks to Mother, who aches in the knees on account of all the running we've done, in the middle of the night, straight into nothing.

"You know what nothing is?" she'll ask me. "Nothing is dark light. It's black noise. It's the only way I knew to save you."

I want to give my mother Kepler—the best of him from me. I want to make her misery end, help her toward believing that there's no use running anymore. The No Good is gone. We lost it. We're free. Give your knees a rest, I want to tell Mother. Unlock the doors and breathe.

Johannes Kepler was born with the skies in his eyes, I write at last, the first words of the essay. *He was born looking up so he could see.* I smudge the facts, to make the opening sing, but now I settle into the truths as I find them in the tepee of books on my bed. *Kepler was a sick baby, and a poor one,* I write on. *He was almost a Lutheran and never a Catholic, which wasn't good where he came from. Still, Kepler was a genius and everyone who met him knew it, and it didn't take him long at all to become the Imperial Mathematician.*

Imperial. My mother will like that.

Outside, Harvey's going crazy in the alley. I finish my thought and set my pen aside, then run the stairs to the attic. I slide in across the crossbeams and take my place at the window. It's the crows that have Harvey in a stir, the bunch of them back in the tree, and now I hear Miss

Cloris calling, "Harvey, you let those birds be." She stands on her porch wearing red shorts and a khaki-colored tee, a loose kerchief on her head. She wears a pale-yellow apron and holds a wooden spoon high in one hand, and when she talks to Harvey, she waves the spoon like she's conducting his circus.

"You get in here, Harvey Rudd," she says, but the dog pays her no mind, and the crows don't show much interest one way or the other: they are busy with their tree play. Now when Miss Cloris looks up, toward the tree of crows, her eyes get stuck on me.

"Why, Sophie Marks," she says. "Good morning to you."

"Good morning, Miss Cloris."

"You busy over there?"

"Working on Kepler."

She swishes her spoon for a second or two, then "Aren't you an interesting one?" she says.

"Homework," I tell her. "An essay for Mother."

"You learning celestial mechanics?"

"Learning Kepler," I say.

"I like that," Miss Cloris says. She makes a funny little down strike with her spoon, then smiles wide. "You need a break, you come on over," she says. "I'm making custard for Miss Helen, and with custard, there's always extra."

"Yes, ma'am."

"Harvey means to apologize for the noise."

"That's all right."

"I'm afraid that there will be no taming Harvey."

"Maybe he just likes birds," I say.

"Maybe that's so."

"Maybe he just likes the big outside."

"Now, that's the truth. You need a break, you know what to do."

"Thank you, ma'am."

"Otherwise, you carry on with Kepler. Perhaps you'll share your findings when you're done?"

"You'd like that?"

"Now, don't get silly with me, Sophie Marks. We like our learning at the Joey Rudd house."

From Nothing to Big Things, I think. From No One to Someone. It's a whole wide world out there.

Emmy

⊗   ⊗   ⊗   ⊗

I fit my right arm along the long shelf of Arlen's shoulder and lean in, trust Arlen, let him take us on through the station door. There is jitter in my bones, jitter and weight upon my heart. Up ahead, the station doors open and close, and we are three steps away; we are two.

"You okay?" Arlen asks.

I feel like a fever.

"We should rest a bit," Arlen says. "I recommend it."

Through the high-up windows of the station, cones of sun fight their way in.

"Baby has jewels for eyes," I remind Arlen, so he knows what he is looking for. "Baby smells like Baby." I see her going back and coming near in the backyard swing beneath the sky above the green ant jungle. I feel the feather touch of her almost hair, sense her head bob on my shoulder. She is near. She must be near. And she is mine, nobody else's.

"We'll rest a bit," Arlen says. "And then we'll search."

The clutch of his hand at my waist. The leaned-into ache of his shoulders. I scan the room for Baby. Scan the pews. Scan the sunbeams. Scan the shadows. Where?

From the sour smell of a cardboard box, a kitten pokes its furred head. From the polished wood of the waiting-room pews spill crates and luggage, shoes and hands, a jacket slung and a woman curved, her profile sliced by the sun. There are three girls playing jacks. There is that man with that dog.

"Sit awhile, Emmy. Get your bearings."

I can't move without Arlen. I can't go up and down between the pews, can't find my way into the blue of shadows nor get near to the farthest corner by the ladies' washroom, where the secrets of the station spool. On the signboards, the trains are laid out in their order—the name of the train, the departing time, the destination city. Up against one wall runs the slender ticket counter, with the agents lined up behind bars. Beyond the back doors the red caps stand, behind the smoke veil of cigarettes and fuel. Overhead, the speakers blare Washington, D.C.; New York City; Boston; Harrisburg; and here comes the lady in green, oozing up toward the ticket counter. She moves as if the air were made of honey. She carries the blade of a rose in one hand, a yellow rose, and touches the head of a boy in summer plaid; she is alone. When the clock above the signboard clicks 7:47, the station becomes chaos and time.

"No harm," Arlen says, "in sitting still for just one moment."

Where Arlen goes I can go. Where he won't I cannot. Across the farthest distance, near the ladies' washroom, on the far other side of things, a woman in white paces a short distance. Her skirt swishes. It nicks and swirls. She walks into a sunbeam and out of a sunbeam, over and over again. "Harrisburg," the blare says. "Last call." And now again the woman turns, and this time when she does, I see how her arms are shaped into a hollow and how inside that hollow is bounce and tremble. She walks and her skirt swishes. She walks and she bobbles her parcel. She walks and she is nervous, back and forth, and all of a sudden, in the crackle of waiting and watching, I smell Baby. Absolutely.

"Arlen!" I say. "Arlen! It's her! Her and my Baby!"

I point, and he stares. I point, and he won't move, and the lady's skirt swishes in the pearl light of the beamed sun; her arms hold Baby. "Arlen!" I call out. "What's the matter with you? Look!"

But Arlen won't move. He shakes his head and says, "That's just a woman, Emmy, not a thief," and I say, "Arlen, that's a woman stealing Baby!" His hand is claw and his arm is pressure. He nooses me into himself.

"You're seeing things."

"Don't do this, Arlen," I say. "Don't ruin me and my Baby." I hop and he holds me, and now with the hand with which I have been pointing, I make a fist and I pound at whatever part of him I can. "Look," I say, and he squints and I squint, and now the sun is all of a sudden all wrong, leveling a haze down in that far corner.

Arlen says, and I hear the words, and the words are

wrong: "Emmy. Love. Listen to me. It's just your imagination."

"I saw something, Arlen. I smelled it. Smelled Baby." Pounding my hand on his chest, pointing in Baby's direction.

"Emmy, it's all right. We'll find her." He wrestles with me, won't let me go.

"We already have!"

"There's no one there. There's nothing but sun."

And suddenly I don't hear the overhead blare. Suddenly the sunspots burn, and the faraway corner is fuzz and blur. A crowd has gathered, and over the sound of Arlen talking, there's the sound of another kind of hurry. There's blare in the streets and blare coming through, someone saying my name, Mrs. Rane. "We have a situation, Mrs. Rane."

"Leave me!" I scream. "It's her! It's the thief who has my Baby!" But now it isn't Arlen's hands but another pair of hands upon me, and I hear Sergeant Pierce on his walkie-talkie: "Suspect's been found. We're taking her in." I feel my arms pulled back behind me, the slap of two cuffs on my wrists.

"Back off, now. Back away," the sergeant says, and I can't see and I can't feel whomever he is talking to, and I can only hear Arlen, loud, Arlen defensive: "Sir! She means no harm. She is a mother."

There's another sergeant and he gathers up my feet. There's a crowd and it breaks. I am carried from the station like a sling.

Sophie

❈   ❈   ❈   ❈

"It's the nutmeg," Miss Cloris is saying, "that makes it special. You ever have nutmeg?"

"Not that I know of, ma'am."

"Born of a tree," she says. "The *Myristica fragrans.* Now, isn't that some name for a tree?"

"Nice as *acacia.*"

"Sure is. Here. Have another."

The custard's the color of eggs and milk browned over by spice. Miss Cloris baked it and set it to cool inside a dozen dishes, each one no bigger than my palm. I could eat custard all day. I could take a bath in it. Miss Cloris blows a soft whistle up through the puffy parts of her hair and asks me to tell her about Kepler. I pause and think, recite the essay's first sentence. She whistles again, closes her eyes.

"'Johannes Kepler was born with the skies in his eyes,'" she repeats. "You wrote that yourself?"

I nod.

"Didn't find it in a book somewhere?"

I shake my head no.

"You know what we call that, don't you?"

"What?"

"We call that talent. Here," she says. "Have another custard."

I feel my face go red and dig my spoon in deep and let the sweet smooth taste cover my tongue. "Miss Helen's recipe," Miss Cloris says.

"Where is Miss Helen?"

"Coming to us when she's ready, as she does."

"She isn't ready?"

"Miss Helen needs her rest, God be blessing Miss Helen."

"Yes, ma'am."

On the floor, at my feet, Harvey yips. He knocks his tail against the linoleum tile and lets his tongue fall free. Miss Cloris says Harvey is not a fan of custard. She's got him busy with a bone. "So what's next?" she asks. "After your first sentence?"

"'He was born looking up so he could see.'"

"Is that a fact?"

"It could have been."

"My word," Miss Cloris says, licking her own custard spoon. "Your mother has some Kepler coming. When does she get home?"

"Around five o'clock."

"How much more essay writing are you planning on?"

"Some."

"We're not here to interfere with your learning, Sophie."

"You're not, Miss Cloris—I promise."

I look away from her and around the room, take notice of the pictures on the high parts of the walls—painted cardboard cutouts inside boxes. It's Alice big and small. The Queen of Hearts. The White Rabbit. The Walrus and the falling Humpty Dumpty. Tweedledum and Tweedledee.

"My Wonderland dioramas," Miss Cloris explains without me asking. "It's a bit of a fetish."

"Did you make them?"

"I did not. That would be Miss Helen's talent."

"She makes Wonderland pictures?"

"It's been a long time, dear. But yes, she once did. That's the story of us, as a matter of fact. I met Miss Helen at her Wonderland booth at a country crafts fair. I couldn't take my eyes off her dioramas."

"I thought you were sisters," I say, confused. "Aunt and aunt?"

"We're Joey's aunts," Miss Cloris says. "But that doesn't mean we're sisters. Here. Let me show you something." She pushes back from the table and walks across the room. She pulls a picture from the wall, a pencil drawing, brings it to me, sits down again.

"That you?" I ask.

"It was."

"With eyes like that? That hair?"

"Time washes over, changes the look of things. But that's not the point I was making. My point was, Miss Helen drew this. Miss Helen is an artist. Was when I met her and always had been. I fell for her Wonderland dioramas."

I nod, confused, and Miss Cloris's face gets far away—the look in her eyes, the smile not for me. "You ever been to Wonderland?" she asks me now.

"No, ma'am," I say.

"Don't deny yourself, you hear me?"

She is looking past me now, over my shoulder, and I turn, too, to the creak of Miss Helen's bamboo wheelchair, which Miss Helen with her own strength is rolling forward, her hands on the thin rubber wheels. She comes from the sky room down the hall. When she gets close enough to the kitchen table, she lifts her arms, like one of those flopping puppets my mother used to parade across the ledge of the couch in whatever rooms we then were living.

"Aren't you a sight for sore eyes?" Miss Cloris says, standing now to wheel Miss Helen the rest of the way in, to the table. Harvey lifts his head and yips, then settles his jaw back onto his front paws.

"I'm afraid I overslept the party."

"Not at all," Miss Cloris says. "The custard had to set. And Sophie just got here, besides." She finds a spoon for

Miss Helen, hands her a bowl of custard. She stands there hovering and won't sit down until Miss Helen has her first taste of the stuff.

"Heaven on earth," Miss Helen says, swallowing slowly. "I thank you for it." She's wearing a pale-peach dress with a scooped round neck and sleeves that come down just past her shoulders and that hair, which is a long, smooth sameness of white. It's her hands I notice, art-making hands, younger than the rest of her.

"Our newest neighbor has been writing on Kepler," Miss Cloris says now.

"Is that right?"

"Writing like a poet, might I add."

"I would have guessed that."

"Tell her your first sentence, Sophie," Miss Cloris urges. "Don't be shy." And when I repeat myself a second time, Miss Helen closes her eyes and smiles.

"Oh my," she says, "you fit right in here. How in the world did you get yourself on Kepler?"

"By way of the Archimedean solids," I say, but when Miss Helen and Miss Cloris exchange funny glances, I trade my answer for another. "By way of my mother," I say. "She has a thing for Kepler."

"And right she should," Miss Cloris says. "He was a smart man."

"Also Imperial," I say.

"Is that a fact?"

"That's an actual fact," I assure them.

"We like facts of all kinds." Miss Helen smiles. She's eaten halfway through her cup of custard and stopped. Miss Cloris has been watching her, and now I watch her watch.

"Eat a little more now, Helen," she tells her. "For strength."

"I'm afraid I'm already full."

"Honey," Miss Cloris says, "do it for me," and slow but sweet, Miss Helen obliges—lifts the spoon to the O of her mouth and takes a long time swallowing. "Custard's good for the soul," Miss Cloris tells her.

"And delicious," Miss Helen says. "Absolutely." The words come out like the back end of a sigh. She puts her spoon down and Harvey yawns. "You bad old dog," she says in a loving voice. She closes her eyes but doesn't close her smile. Miss Cloris fits her hand over hers.

"I best be going," I say now, standing, remembering my mother's Kepler and her rules, and thinking how Miss Helen needs Miss Cloris to coax her through another custard or two, and how I should not be here. Harvey raises his eyebrows at me but doesn't yip. Miss Helen says I should stay until Joey gets home, but I'm decided. Around the table I go, to give Miss Helen a kiss. I let Miss Cloris walk me through to the door.

———

"She'll be all right," Miss Cloris says, as if I asked her.

"I know," I say, but I don't.

"You write your heart out on Kepler," Miss Cloris says, "and return with the news."

"I'll do what I can," I say. "That's my best method."

Part Two

Emmy

A room that isn't mine. The sound of toss and dream, and sheets like the fried bottom of a pan. At the far end of the room, in a square: sun like it's been poured into a glass of milk and swallowed—a blank face in a square space of scratch and rake and air clot. I will be smothering down to nothing.

Fix it, Emmy. Think. Remember.

A woman with a white skirt whishing. Train eyes on the train tracks, coming. The rain coming down, and I am rescued. In the back of a car, in a room with a bulb—bare and too bright and banging, and the bulb is swinging, it is blinding, and who is the man asking questions? The two men? Peter? Is Peter asking questions?

"Nothing you have done can be explained."

Someone has Baby.

Nothing you have done.

What have I done? Another room, another man. A flapping blue jacket.

"You were never right in the head."

Where is Baby?

Book says it's right to love your baby.

"Shouldn't have married you for pity, like I done."

"You married me for my cake."

"Married you for your cake? You see how it is, Your Honor? Your ears bear witness? My wife is wrong in the head. She's crazy."

"Order in the court. Order, please. Mr. Rane, you keep your fists down."

The white skirt whishing.

"Mrs. Rane."

"I'm Mrs. Rane."

"For your own good."

"For my own good, what?"

"Order in the court!"

Who'll look for Baby?

"I hereby declare . . ."

Declare?

". . . in light of her breakdown . . ."

Whose breakdown?

". . . or until otherwise remediated."

Thirteen steps up, thirteen steps down, and the dogs barking. What is a mother's first rule? What is? What is? What is?

The man and the world on his handlebars.

Speed and hurry.

Release me. I have done nothing.

Sophie

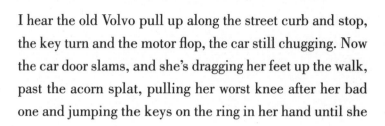

I hear the old Volvo pull up along the street curb and stop, the key turn and the motor flop, the car still chugging. Now the car door slams, and she's dragging her feet up the walk, past the acorn splat, pulling her worst knee after her bad one and jumping the keys on the ring in her hand until she finds the one that fits the door, which I locked myself when I came back home, too early for Joey, in time for Kepler, the good daughter I am, the be-gooder.

"Sophie?" she calls, and I hurry to relieve her of the weight of the Styrofoam boxes she's carried in from the diner. "Turkey meat loaf," she says. "Garlic potatoes." There's heat in them still.

"Not bad," I tell her, like she cooked them herself.

"A little bit of luck, I'd call it, if I hadn't worked so hard to earn it."

"I'll put them in the oven," I say. "Keep them warm."

She heads for the La-Z-Boy, lowers herself in. She levers the footstool, fits her head inside the leatherette wedge. When I return from the kitchen, her eyes are closed, and there's the sound of a far-off train in her nose. I wait for her eyes to open, for the chance to say, *I wrote you a perfection ode to Kepler.* I wait for something. Nothing. I say, "Mother" gently, and her eyes stay closed. I head for the stairs, walk the outside parts, where there's hardly any squeak, leaving the meat loaf and the potatoes in the cold cave of the oven.

"Did you make it up to me?" she asks now, talk from her sleep.

"I did."

"Dinner in an hour," she mumbles.

But the train rolls on, high speed.

Emmy

A wheeled chair at the end of the bed. One woman, then another coming. "Six weeks for the ankle," the one says, leaning in, snapping the spring on the clipboard someone tied—how long ago?—to the metal post of this bed. "A month for the arm. You've banged yourself good." She goes away and she comes back—teeth straight as boxcars, hair chopped off at the ears, high egg of a head. Her eyes are like hyphens between the broken part of words. Her nose is a man's nose, the wrong kind.

"What's the wheels for?" I ask now, my voice crunchy.

"For taking a ride in," she says. Leaves the clipboard hanging from its string, leans in over the foot end of my bed, snaps the sheets off my legs. The dust goes for a crazy swim over the bare bones of all the others, over their glass bottles and their feeding tubes, their sour pans, their sheets thrown to the floor, their moaning, a sound like a tunnel through my ears. Days now. Weeks? How long?

When the tall one smiles, her mouth makes an upside-down U and the blonde beside her smiles, too, except that her smile goes side to side and stops short. "Scoot along, now," the blonde says, and now she says it again, as if I don't understand *scoot*, and they both of them reach in and pinch me up under my arms, scrunch me toward them.

"What are you doing?" I demand. "Leave me be!" But they are busy—hauling and pinching and lifting, and the chair rides on the wheels. "Won't do you any good, this fighting," the tall one says. My eyes go in and out of blur. My head is dizzy. When I'm into the chair, they turn me, and I am going to be sick, the way I once was sick on the up-down swirl of a merry-go-round.

I hear the sounds of tossed sheets, and moans. I hear the ricochet of words across this room that is bed after bed after bed, and the milk light is streaming through. It's the blonde who makes the wheeled chair move beneath me, who takes me bump bump bump over the broken tiles of the floor, my bones breaking all over again at each slam and pop.

"Where are you taking me?" I ask.

"To privileges," the blonde says. As if she says that every day. As if it means something.

"Privileges?"

"That's right?"

"What's privileges look like?"

"A room with a door."

"What kind of room doesn't have a door?"

They laugh above my head. Ha, ha. The other one, the bigger one, stops laughing. "You earn your privileges," she tells me. "You earn them, or you lose them. Privileges is obeying. It is excellent good behavior."

Excellent good? What is excellent good? One of the wheels on this chair is a flat squat lump. The chair goes bump bump bump, and my ankle's angry. The stitch up my arm feels like a lit stick of something. We're through the door of the long room and out into a hall, and the hall is longer than the long room was and the ceiling is low and the bulbs are orange. On either side of the hall are benches, and from the benches murmurs mist, and down the hall, a thin man with a pail mops dirty water into a corner, smelling like lemon and bleach.

"You understand, Emmy?" the blonde one asks.

"Excuse me?"

"Privileges is obeying."

"Morning, Miss Granger," the mop man says.

"Morning, Julius," the tall one with the egg head says.

"Morning, Bettina."

"That's a nice shine you're putting onto the floor," Bettina answers.

The hallway is linoleum, a used-up yellow. The tiles go bump. The women walking or waiting or sleeping on the benches wear their dresses loose at their shoulders, their hair in knots. Now with my good arm and hand I reach up to touch my own, to smooth it down. I wear the same dress as the rest of them. I wear it pale blue and thin, and I wonder where my Levis are, where my comb is, Baby's sock. "Tell me the what for," I say.

"Excuse me?" the one called Granger answers.

"Whose rules? What country?"

"You'll get the hang of it," Bettina says, as if I'm to get used to this, like this is not some mistake, as if Baby isn't out there, waiting for me, trusting me to find her. I feel the swimmy whoosh like the early days of Baby being tucked inside. "I'm going to be sick," I say. The bad tire goes smack against the upped tile of a linoleum block and my ankle bangs.

"If you were well," Granger says, "you wouldn't be here."

"I mean it," I say, but Granger pulls a file from her pocket. Rounds a nail, chews back its flesh.

Sophie

❀　　　❀　　　❀　　　❀

The moon is shrinking. The stars lie low above the thread of clouds. Cicadas talk in the grass and the crows rustle and Mother never woke to my Kepler.

"Mother?" I asked. "Mom?"

"Tomorrow," she mumbled, and now, looking out on the dark of the world, I remember afternoons when I made my mother happy, when we were safe again, in another new house, when the No Good couldn't find us. We cut dolls from doilies and pasted them on sticks, and it would be her turn first, and then it would be mine, to tell our most magnificent stories. My stories were sister stories. Her stories were adventures. Her life as a barracuda hunter. Her rocket rides to the moon. The year she lived with a giraffe in her pantry and an elephant in her living room. Back then her hobble was a small hobble and her hair was like a paintbrush run against my skin when she leaned in close to play.

"Mother," I tried again. "I finished the Kepler."

"It should be good," she said. "Is it good?"

"It's for you."

"We'll let it sit, then," she said. "Until tomorrow."

In the house across the alley, at the kitchen table, Miss Cloris sits with a violet apron on, and Joey feeds Harvey with his fingers, and I can't see Miss Helen but I know that she's there, from the way Miss Cloris bends and leans, lifting Minxy from the floor with the jiggling O of her arms and setting her down on a wheelchaired pair of knees. Joey's cap fights the curls on his head. He wears his shoes untied and his shorts loose, and it's homework he's working over, books he turns the pages of while he feeds Harvey with his fingers. If he would just turn around, he would see me.

Joey. Turn around and see me.

But now Harvey has jumped his two front paws to Joey's knees. He's running his tongue along the shelf of Joey's chin, scrambling his back paws across the tile floor as if he's trying to jump them, too, as if he's a lap-size Minxy. Joey closes his book and makes room. He reaches down and scruffs Harvey's fur, and suddenly the big dog's there, king of the kitchen table, yelping so proud and loud that even from here I can hear him.

Turn around, I think, *and see me,* and now I hear the near muffle of somebody crying, and I turn back to the dark and the pink of the floor and the splintering of the beams, and nobody's up here but me.

Emmy

"I told you," I say when it is done, when all I want is a fresh Saltine to clear the slosh taste from my mouth.

"Thank God for Julius," Granger says.

"That's three times this week that someone lost it on my watch," Bettina says. "I'm in line for better times."

"You and me both," Granger tells her, and I try to picture her above me now, but all I can picture are her two eye hyphens. Elevator doors slide open, and Bettina pushes me inside, turns me around, hits 4. There's an old stool below the buttons, and Granger sits, pulls out her file, checks her nail. There's a dark stain on the elevator floor and a quilted mattress above, its ends drooping down like an old cloud, and when the elevator climbs, I feel the sink of the emptiness inside. In the steel face of the doors, I watch Bettina pulling a hoop through the hole in her ear. When the elevator pings and the doors slide apart, it's Bettina who puts her weight against my chair and rolls me through.

"Four thirty-three A," Granger says now, pulling a piece of paper from the pocket in her skirt.

"This should be interesting," Bettina says, and we roll, and now the floor is concrete and it's the cracks that hurt and the only thing I see, miles on end, is steel doors with thick windows, steel knobs. At 433, we stop. Bettina slips a bracelet of keys from her wrists, finds the right one, turns the lock. "Welcome home," she says.

"This isn't home," I say.

"This is privileges," Granger says. "Better get accustomed."

But all I see is the thin nothing of a cot and the long draw of a dark blue curtain that slices the room in two. At the end of the room is a chest of drawers—four fat drawers, one skinny—and on the top of the chest sits a plastic globe wearing a crown of pink goggles.

"Autumn?" Bettina calls, talking to the side of the curtain I can't see.

"Yes, ma'am."

"Autumn. You come say hello."

"Hello," I hear, and then whoever she is giggles, her voice squeaking like a horn in tune-up. She doesn't pull the curtains back. I can see nothing but shadows.

"Use your manners, Autumn."

"I said 'ma'am,' didn't I?"

"You know what I mean."

I hear the creak of a bed. I hear another blow of giggles. Finally Granger walks to the curtain and snaps it back, and there Autumn is, standing on her own thin cot in a gray T-shirt and a red puff skirt, throwing a ridiculous curtsy. Through the small round of the window behind her, the sun comes in, and where it hits her hair, there's a burst of yellow orange.

"What happened to you?" she asks me.

"Be nice," Bettina tells her.

"It's a question," Autumn says, "is all." And now she curtsies again, pinches the red puff up into her skinny fingers, cracks her legs at her knees, and says, her voice gone solemn, "Welcome to State."

I nod, but when I nod, my teeth start to chatter, and now Bettina and Granger, no warning, scoop me up from the chair and lay me down on the cot. The sheets smell like some other person.

"Roomie number seven," Autumn declares, queen-like, and I close my eyes so that I can't listen, so that everything around me goes to mumbles. All I see is Baby, and how much Baby needs me. Baby and her yellow sock, the little knobs of bone that are her ankles.

"You rest up, now," Bettina says, stepping away now, seeing Granger out before she closes the door behind her. "And Autumn, you know the rules. Let her be."

The door shuts. The lock turns. The elevator pings down the hallway. The cot beneath the curtsy creaks. It's Autumn's feet sweeping the floor.

"Lucky you," she says.

Lucky *me*?

"They got you your own special chair and everything."

She slides into the plastic seat and I peel my left eye open. She's nearly bent in two as she studies the gadgets, her poufy skirt spilling everywhere. She has a Band-Aid on one elbow, a bruise on her knee. "You need a chauffeur?" she asks. "For getting places?"

"I'm not staying here," I tell her. "Not staying long."

"Between now and then, then," she says. As if it's decided.

Sophie

❋　　　❋　　　❋　　　❋

"Mother," I say. "Mother, what's wrong?"

"Exhaustion," she says, like the word is a mile long. She must have iced her knees in the middle of the night, because parts of the La-Z-Boy swim and parts of it leak and the two plastic bags are knocked to the floor like balloons whizzed empty. Her name runs ninety degrees wrong on her cashier outfit. Her collar is crushed and stained. Her hair has gone whiter overnight, the white hair yawning away from her head.

"Have you eaten, Mother?" I ask her.

"Not since yesterday, noon."

"You have to keep your strength up," I tell her. "Remember?" I head for the kitchen and the Styrofoam boxes, open the cold oven door. The turkey meatloaf has turned to cardboard in the oven; the potatoes are stones. "Milk?" I ask her, coming back, standing above her, because we have that, we have milk at least, which I can serve her hot or cold. But she says no. "Rice?" I ask. "Tomatoes?" From the people who lived here before.

"Not today, Sophie."

"I'll go out," I say, "and get something."

"You will not."

"You aren't well, Mother. Let me do something."

"Just sit here, Sophie. Tell me a story."

"A story?"

"Didn't you say you were working on Kepler? Read it to me, what you have."

"Now, Mother?"

"When else? I am your audience."

She smiles, and her smile is thin blue. She looks at me, and her dark eyes mist. Outside, the crows are busy in the tree and the bees swarm and the acorns are back at their battle, splatting the hard gray slate walk. Mother's next shift is the eight o'clock shift, and here she is, feet up, name crooked, La-Z-Boy growing beneath her like a lake. "We need to get you ready," I say.

"I'm calling it in."

"Calling it in?"

"I need a break, Sophie. I can't stand there, with my knees like this, splitting their dollars with change."

"It's a new job, Mother. It's your work. Don't you say, 'New job, best effort'? Isn't that your motto?"

"I've done my best, and they'll understand, and if they don't, then it's a big too bad."

"Too bad for who, Mother?"

"Too bad for *whom*ever. Exhaustion like this, you can't

fight it." She closes her eyes and goes back and forth with her head in the leatherette neck rest, as if she's shaking off a dream or bad weather. She lifts one hand and reaches for me. I pretend that I don't see.

"You'll feel better after you eat," I say, heading for the pantry, for a box of rice, for the can of soupy tomatoes, a little round rust across the top.

"I need to sleep, Sophie. Sleep. Don't bother in the kitchen."

"But, Mother." I grab the rice box and read the instructions. I find the measuring cup, the stick of butter. I pull the pot from the lazy Susan drawer, and Mother calls out to me, "What did I say, now, about bothering?"

"Strength," I say.

"It'll be like old times," she says. "You and me, Sophie. A day off. A spontaneous together."

But it's not old times; it's now. It's the Rudds next door and my heart tugging on lemonade and custard, acacia and Cather, Joey owing me the pitch and the wild sweet of his curls. Mother can't lie here all day, saying she wants Kepler and not wanting Kepler and not planning to keep to her business, which is leaving for work so that I can leave this place, too. She cannot. I spigot the water into the measuring cup, put the pot on the stove, dial around to medium high.

"I'm not eating any rice," she warns me. "Not at seven in the morning, I'm not."

"What else, then?" I ask. "Tell me what else."

"Warm me some milk," she says. "But not yet. I need to wake to it."

"You're not awake?"

"I'm resting, Sophie, if you don't mind. As if I haven't earned it. As if . . ."

"We're halfway to rice here, Mother. According to the instructions."

"I'd prefer milk," she says. "Warm. In an hour. Milk, when I'm ready, would be better. Bring me the phone, will you? The cord's long enough for the stretch."

"You're calling it in?"

"Have you been listening, Sophie? To what I'm saying?"

"You're going to sit here all day?"

"Until I can stand up, I will."

"But, Mother. What will happen then?"

"Have I not taken care of you, Sophie? From the start, have I not? Have I not earned your trust?"

"But, Mother."

"Warm milk," she says. "In an hour."

The priest in the hills, I think. The custard like ice cream. Joey to school and Joey home, and my mother sitting here.

Emmy

When I wake, she's still there, at the end of my cot, haunched up on the wheeled chair, rubbing my casted foot with tiny fingers.

"They were turning blue," she tells me, meaning the toes, I guess, stuck out over the boot of the cast. I feel little sizzles wherever her fingers go. I feel cold when her touch works away, my teeth still chattering.

"Who are you, anyway?" I ask her, shivering. She's thrown a sweater over her shoulders, a silver sequined thing with all but a lonely button missing.

"Autumn," she says. "You already forget?"

"I wasn't meaning your name," I say. I look up, and the ceiling is those ceiling tiles, like school. I look to the walls, which are gray. I look over the sheets, which are brown. I look to the crown of goggles on the globe. I keep the tears where they are, not falling.

"What were you meaning, then?"

"Just, you know: Who?"

She says nothing for a long time, staring—the side of her hair catching the window sun all lit up and the other side curling past her shoulders. She's got freckles in the valleys beneath her eyes and fringe lashes. She's got ears too big for her head. She's the thinnest girl I've ever seen, the part stuck above her elbows thin as the part that swings below.

"I am the luckiest thing that ever happened to you, that's who," she says, then blows through the horn of her giggle. "Psshhhahh," she says, shaking her head. "Didn't no one tell you? I'm the only genius at State."

"The only one?"

She smiles and her smile is a big upside-right U. "I never lie," she says, raising her arms quick as a surprise, then dropping them quicker so that she can spin herself a whole circle in the chair, like she's been practicing her spin work while I've been sleeping. "Cool wheels," she says when she's done.

"Wheel's broken."

"You don't like broken things, you shouldn't be here."

"That's right," I say. "I shouldn't." I feel the first tear fall and then the next one. I swat them away. They keep coming. Autumn stares at me, and then she watches the sun, the milk of it pouring through the thick-as-walls window.

"You're in for a ride now," she says at last, "rooming with me." She spins—one, two, three—then stops. Dead, cold, perfect stop. Something with her hands she does, something with her feet, to make the wheeled chair start and stop. "You know why I'm so good at this?" she asks.

"Don't know." My voice sounds funny, like it's full of side-walk cracks.

"It's my pilot training," she says. "Also my skydiving."

"Is that a fact?" My tongue sticks and unclicks from the roof of my mouth.

"Most certainly is."

"You wear pouf skirts when you're flying?"

"I wear whatever I want."

"How come?"

"How come what?"

"They let you wear that, and I'm wearing this?" I look down at the thin bit of nothing they put me in. A dress tied with strings at the back, no collar. Degradations, is what it is. Wronged up and uglied. Stolen from.

"Infirmary tricked you out," she says. Starts laughing. Stops.

"Where are my real clothes?"

"Heck if I know."

"I need my real clothes," I tell her. "So I can get out."

Her eyes go sky wide. "You leaving? So soon?"

"Best as I can."

She stares at me, screws up her nose, too little a nose for all its freckles. "Me, too," she says finally. "Leaving right with you. Up. And. Out." She whirls herself, makes a circle. She slumps down, makes like exhaustion. "I have a degree in the color blue," she says. "And once"—and now she leans in toward me, plants her elbows to the right edge of my bed— "I fell through nine completely separate clouds in a single afternoon, a world record. Don't believe me, look it up. You will find it to be true." She points at the globe behind her with the goggle crown, like that's proof enough of her story.

"What are you doing here, then?" I ask her, the way I would have asked the snobby girl in school, back when there was school, back when I had choices and made the wrong one.

"Big mistake," she says. "Right same as you." And there's nothing I can say to that, and nothing I say, period.

"So. You going to tell me now?"

"Tell you what?"

"How you banged yourself so pretty? You fall from the sky? You forget your chute?"

"I can't," I say. "I can't tell you."

Her eyes go wide, so blue. "Is it a secret, what you can't tell?"

"Worse than a secret," I say, and I don't know why I say it, why I confess, to Autumn, the crazy and the skinny, but when I say it, when I know it to be true, the tears start coming and they will not stop and suddenly I am howling animal howls and suddenly I am screaming and I am yelling at Peter, and I am yelling for Baby, and I am yelling at Arlen to find her, Arlen, who thought he could save me, who wouldn't believe me, who stood there afterward, yelling, "I'm so sorry." I see everything that was and everything that's wrong and all the people in the world who could have Baby and what are they doing to Baby? Where is my Baby? How many houses in the whole wide world will I have to search through to find Baby? And now Autumn goes to blur and she's gone, and now she's beside me—down the narrow rim of the bed, lying near. I know that it's her. I smell her hair. She holds me strong as a thin girl has no right to.

"You can tell me," she says into my ear, but I can't, can't even breathe, and now she takes the fingers of my ruined arm and counts them, one two three four five one two three four five one two three four five, until I can breathe and I am not so close to drowning.

"I have worse than secrets, too," she whispers, and that's all she says, and then we lie there like that, together on the bed, her frizzy hair my pillow, her count the way I breathe, until from outside, in the long hall, I hear Bettina calling.

"What is going on in here?" she demands, bursting through.

"She needs me," Autumn says.

"Julius reported a ruckus."

"There was no ruckus."

"Don't lie to me, Autumn. Do you hear me?"

"It wasn't her," Autumn says. "I swear it wasn't. She's been sleeping." And she's holding me tight, and I'm counting to myself, one two three four five one two three four . . .

Sophie

❈　　❈　　❈　　❈

She stays home and stays home, lives in that chair.
Drinks the milk warm, eats the rice cold, gets up only and
slowly to pee or to run her finger down the crack in the
curtains, then throw the curtains tight again, as if she's
being hunted by weather, as if being hunted makes her so
tired out that all she can do is sit back down in that chair.
Sometimes, after three, the Rudd door slams and Harvey
slides across the porch with his long scraping paw nails,
and then the door will slam again and it will be the sound
of Joey thumping down the alley. "For the love of God,"
Mother will moan, "will they be quiet?" It'll take her a
long time to settle, but she does, and when that happens,
I tiptoe up the stairs, rush across the pink, throw my head
out the window toward Joey, whispering, "Hey," until he
looks up and says, "Hey," in a soft shout right back, and
after that, today, he says, "How is she?"

"Sick," I say. "Real sick."

"Sleeping sick or awake sick?"

"Little of sleeping and awake."

Joey bounces the ball and Harvey steals it. Harvey

skiddles across the alley and then returns, dropping the ball at Joey's feet. Joey retrieves it, turns, and pitches hard, and Harvey barrels down the alley so fast that his legs get in the way.

"We're holding the Cather on you," Joey tells me.

"You're doing that?"

"Aunt Helen insisted. Says she'll dream on it until you return. She doesn't want you missing out on the story."

"You'll give her my thanks?"

"You come over here and give it. She's missing you."

"But I'm just right here."

"Three stories up. Like Rapunzel." Joey shadows his eyes and squints. "You should grow your hair, at least, so I could climb it."

"That was a fairy tale," I say. "You can't climb hair." I laugh, and then Joey's laughing, and then, remembering my mother downstairs, I say, "Shhh," with a finger to my lips.

"It's an idea, anyway," Joey says in a whisper-shout. Harvey has returned the ball and dropped it at Joey's feet. He squeaks like a wheel and waits for the pitch, until Joey delivers a nice long one and the dog's off. "You should call a doctor," Joey says now, "if your mother's so sick."

"She wouldn't have it."

"Why not?"

"She's a private person."

"So what?"

"It's complicated."

"You should have Aunt Cloris take a look. She's half a nurse or something."

Harvey returns the ball, and now Joey starts tossing it high—up above his head toward the clouds. Harvey runs in circles. Higher and higher, Joey tosses the ball. If my arms were forty feet long, I'd reach and swipe the soaring thing clean out of the sky.

"Sophie?" I hear now from down below. "Sophie Marks?"

"Joey," I whisper-shout. "That's my mother." I wave my hands, but he's too busy with the ball, too coiled up in Harvey's barking, and even when I lean out far as I can go over the window ledge, he doesn't see or hear me. He tosses the ball and tosses the ball, and Harvey grows wilder at his feet, and my mother keeps calling me, louder. I close the window: snap. I hurry across the beams, tiptoe the outside of the attic stairs, then walk-run the rest of the way down the stairwell's center, making as much noise as I can so it'll sound like I'm coming from the bedroom. Outside, I hear Harvey going wild. Inside, I hear my mother, and when I reach the first floor and glance toward the La-Z turtle, it's empty. She stands by the front door at the window wearing her white nightgown, her hair streaming down her shoulders, her one hip jutting. She's split the curtain by just a crack. In the angle of sun, dust hangs.

"Were you sleeping?" she asks without turning.

"No, ma'am." My heart's up in my throat; it's pounding. I think of all the what-ifs, the consequences. What if she'd parted the curtain on the alley side and not the street side, seen Joey looking up, talking to someone? What if she'd come up the stairs dragging her knee, and I didn't hear her? What if she turns around right now and sees the lying in my eyes and says, "We're moving"?

"You sure took a long time coming," she tells me now.

"Maybe, come to think of it, I was sleeping. Maybe I was."

"Were you or were you not?"

"At the very least, I was daydreaming."

"Your mother's sick," she says, turning and rolling her eyes at my mixed-up confessions. "Have some heart." She faces back toward the window and sighs as if it's my fault all these days are wasting.

I cut toward her, across the room, and stop. I feel the dust bits on my skin, close my mouth tight. I wait for Mother to say something more. She doesn't. She stares instead.

"I wouldn't have moved in here," she says at last, "if I had known about that dog."

"He just gets excited," I say, and then add, at once, to correct myself, "I mean I guess."

She turns, looks over her shoulder, stares me down. "There are no excuses," she says in a low voice, "for an

animal like that." She makes sure that I understand, then
turns back toward the window, wobbles, catches herself
against the sill with a pinch of both hands. The sun pushes
past her. The dust bits dance.

"Can I get you something?" I ask.

"We're out of supplies," she says, as if I hadn't been
telling her the same thing now for days.

"A glass of water?"

"That would be fine. Except I used up all the ice."

"A glass of plain water," I say. "Coming right up."

It's enough to bring her back into the room, toward the
La-Z-Boy. I help settle her in, then head for the kitchen.

"Sophie?" she calls.

"Yes?"

"Run the water until it's full-force cold."

"I'll do my best."

"Make up new ice."

I blast the water and fill the empty ice-cube tray, slip
it into the cave of the freezer. I fill her glass, shirt-dry
its bottom, present it to her like it's something special—
a magic potion for the queen in her throne. I think of Joey
outside, looking for me in the window. I think of Harvey
and how he's gone suddenly quiet. I would give anything
for Rapunzel hair, or even a mother who works the shifts
she'd promised.

"Now," she says, "where were we?" She drinks and

swallows loudly. She touches the tower of books with her hand, looks confused. "Archimedes?" she asks. "Icosahedrons?"

"Actually, Kepler."

"That's right."

"I wrote a paper."

"Now I remember."

"Would you like for me to read it?"

She swallows the last of her water, sighs. "Another time," she says, "when I'm a bit stronger."

We stay silent then—Mother sitting, me standing, the tower of books at her side. Across the alley, they're waiting on Cather. They're also waiting on my Kepler.

"Am I inconveniencing you?" she asks after a while.

"I'm sorry?"

"The look on your face, Sophie. Somewhere between boredom and torture. You'd think after all I've done for you, you could at least . . ."

"Yes, Mother."

"I haven't finished."

"Forgive me, Mother."

She stops, throws up her hand, closes her eyes. "Do what you will," she says at last, surrendering. Her lips are so thin, so gray-blue. She fits one hand to her worse knee.

"What do you need?" I ask her.

"Some sleep," she says. "Uninterrupted."

"All right."

"We've got half the town library sitting on that table," she says, sleepy. "If you're bored, it's your own fault. The whole world's right there."

"Right."

"Right?" But the fight's gone from her, and the train is soon coming, and I know to wait for it, to throw it nowhere off its tracks. I lift the empty water glass from Mother's hand, set it down beside the tower. I steal a story for myself, the thinnest book. I climb the stealthy outside of the stairs, but by the time I reach my attic space, the alley beyond is empty.

Emmy

❦   ❦   ❦   ❦

Dr. Brightman says, "Take a seat." I am on the wheeled chair, already sitting. He says, "EmmyRanesitdownrelax," without looking up to see me. Bettina stays. Granger goes. I wait for Dr. Brightman to take his eyes off the papers on his desk and release me.

"Relax," he repeats.

The wall of my stomach against the strap of the wheeled chair. Bettina at the window, staring.

"Twenty-three," Dr. Brightman says.

"Twenty-three what?"

"Twenty-three days since admission. Four hours out of the infirmary. How are we doing?"

I say nothing. I am not well. He must release me.

"Nervous breakdown and delusions," he says, reading from the chart. "Mrs. Rane?"

"Yes?"

"How are we doing?"

"Dr. Brightman," I say.

"Yes?"

"I'm Emmy Rane."

"That is correct."

"There's been a mistake. I should not be here."

I comb my fingers through my hair to make it neat. I fix the string tie at my neck and sit up proper. If he sees who I am, he will release me. If he understands. Any mother would cry for the want of her baby. Any woman would hate Peter with all her might. Dr. Brightman moves a stack of papers onto another stack of papers. He fiddles around in his shirt pocket, and now here is a pair of horned-rim glasses. Dr. Brightman is an ugly man. His hair is the wrong color. His hair is painted.

"You're having trouble settling in?" he asks.

"Excuse me?"

"You've had an episode?" he says. "According to Bettina?"

"I'm fine."

"You are not fine."

"Of course, sir, I am not fine. Someone is out there with my baby."

"Grave inconsistencies," he says. And then he writes it down.

He wears a watch, its face like the moon. He scratches his forehead with a sausage finger. Outside, beyond the office door, someone is screaming. On the freedom side of the window, the sun is crinkling. "Perhaps we were premature," he says, "in releasing you from the infirmary. Do you think you need more time, Mrs. Rane, in the hospital environment?"

"I do not," I say. "I do not need any more time here at all. What I need is to go find my baby." I pull at the chair's leather strap with my one good hand. I kick at the chair with my casted foot. I think about Autumn, crying when they piled me into the chair, when they leather-strapped me to it. "Don't do it," she was saying. "Don't take her. I can save her." How much time has gone by? Who has been watching? Who is out there, in the woods, on the streets, in the alleys, behind the trees, looking for my baby?

"Bettina?"

"Dr. Brightman?"

"I'm recommending the cleanse."

"The cleanse, sir?"

"The cleanse," he repeats. "And we'll resume the lorazepam. We'll see if that helps, before we return her to infirmary."

"Sir."

"Mrs. Rane," he says, speaking now to me. "This is a team effort. We are at work on your behalf."

"Someone has my Baby." I say it quiet. I say it without kicking. I do not pull at the leather strap. I am well. I have my reason.

"I'll write a scrip," he says. "Send it to the pharmacy."

Sophie

❖　　　❖　　　❖　　　❖

The minute she drags herself across the walk and chuffs down the street, I'm gone—the door slamming behind me, my feet on the slate, my fist against the Rudds' door, pounding.

"What is it, love?" Miss Cloris asks, stepping back, as if I might keep pounding, door or not, even if Harvey's home, prowling, protecting.

"I was just wondering," I say, "if you could use a visit." Beside Miss Cloris, Harvey goes up on his back feet like a dancer, then flops back down. He looks me straight in the eyes, lets his tongue fall loose.

"We could always use a visit," Miss Cloris says. She wears a striped shirt, the purple and red stretching long-wise, over a pair of nubby stretch pants. There's a belt around the barrel of her waist—thin and silver-glittered.

"Can I come in, then?"

"You can."

"Thank you, Miss Cloris."

The air behind her smells of butter, sugar, chocolate. There's a finger stroke of white across her face. She lets me into the first room, then leads me to the kitchen, pulls out a chair, raises an eyebrow. "You're just in time," she says, turning to the counter behind her and piling cookies on a plate and nodding so that I'll take one. It's sweet melt and chocolate chunk. It almost hurts, my hunger.

"It's the Toll House," she says. "Just made."

"Uh-huh."

"Some milk?" she asks.

I nod.

She pours me a quick glass of milk, which fringes to the top with bubbles. She takes an apple from a basket, some crackers from the pantry, a block of cheese from the refrigerator door. "Might as well turn this into a party," she says, and now Minxy arrives from around the corner, snaking her tail and leaping, with no trouble, onto the space above my knees.

"I didn't mean . . . ," I start.

"I've been wanting to taste that cheese," she says, "since I brought it home last Tuesday from the market." She cuts herself a sliver and puts the whole thing in her mouth. She cuts me a wedge and insists.

"We're one shy of a full morning deck," she says, slipping out of the kitchen, around the corner, up the stairs. I cut another wedge of cheese, sandwich it between two crackers. I drink through the bubbles of milk. Finally I hear Miss Cloris on the stairs, and by the time I get to the clean front room, she's halfway down, Miss Helen scooped into her arms like a child. Harvey rushes their ankles faster than I can catch him. When I call him, he listens—lowers his ears and lets the ladies pass.

"I heard we have some company," Miss Helen says. Her voice is small and tired. They reach the bottom of the stairs and stop, Miss Cloris lowering Miss Helen into her special chair. She straightens, combs her fingers through Miss Helen's hair. Now Miss Helen sits and Miss Cloris rolls her and Harvey yips and when they get to the kitchen and are arranged at the table, everyone gets a slice of cheese, even Harvey, who they let me feed with my fingers. Miss Helen tests a cookie—breaks off a piece of a piece, closes her eyes. "You outdo yourself," she tells Miss Cloris, but it's as if Miss Cloris isn't even listening. She's watching Miss Helen, shadows beneath her eyes, and I think, and then I know, that Miss Helen looks smaller since the last of my visits. How many days? She looks smaller and Miss Cloris looks sadder, and suddenly Minxy is back and leaping to my lap, and I feel my stomach start to ache.

"Is she better now?" Miss Helen asks me.

"Ma'am?"

"Your mother. Joey mentioned . . ."

I nod. It's the best I can do.

"You must be a very fine nurse."

"I'm actually no kind of nurse."

"I am surrounded," Miss Helen sighs, "by excessive modesty."

We spend the afternoon on an utmost urgent; that's what Miss Cloris calls it. She goes away, then comes back and says, "We start with doweling rods." Now she's measuring them out—one sixteen inches, the other twenty-four, according to her metal ruler—making a Magic Marker line at both sticks' cutting spots before she knives in and snaps off. When she's done, she rules the sticks out again, putting another mark halfway up the short stick and a third up the long, and when that's done, she holds the two sticks like a cross where the blue dots meet and ties them together with string. Next she notches the sticks' ends, and Miss Helen sighs, and I watch, and I think how sure Miss Cloris is, how nice and neat each cut, and I remember my icosahedron on the kitchen table, not half as nice, not an utmost urgent, Archimedes leading to Kepler leading to silence and my mother sick, and all these days passing, and by the time I finish that thought, Miss Cloris has gone notch to notch with the string and is tying a double knot back up top, and Miss Helen is tired but eager.

"Now," Miss Helen says, "for the fun part."

Miss Cloris goes away and returns with a big cardboard box, which she plonks down to the kitchen floor, scooting Harvey off, but just for a second. "You're such a pooch," she tells the dog, pulling his snout out of her way, unlocking the box flaps and digging in. "Ah, it *is* here," she says, dragging a big sheet of electric-orange fabric up to the table, which Miss Helen, sliding plates and glasses to one side, has made nearly clear.

Miss Cloris smoothes the fabric and lays the wood frame down upon it. She cuts it to the pattern and hands me a bottle of Elmer's. "Outside edges," she says, pointing to the orange diamond, and I squeeze the bottle and smear the glue along the fabric's borders. I check with Miss Cloris, to see how I'm doing. She says, "Don't go shy on the Elmer's." When I'm done, she leans in and shows me what's next—how the orange diamond with its edge of glue is to be pressed to the lengths of string that connect the sticks. I do as she says, and Miss Helen encourages me, until finally the glue and the diamond edge and the string are one thing, and meeting Miss Cloris's satisfaction. She lifts what we've made, holds it high.

"Picture this," she says, "in the sky," and I remember, a long time ago, in a drive from one house to another, seeing a kite on the end of a string, knocking around in the wind. I didn't understand how the kite had gotten there or how it kept its distance from the ground, and I must have asked a million questions, because the next week, when we were settled, Mother came home from the library with a stack of kites-in-stories books. *The Sea-Breeze Hotel. The Dragon*

Kite. The Flyaway Kite. "Kites are better in stories," she said, "than they are in actual life."

"Now comes the best part," Miss Helen is saying while Miss Cloris knots what we have so far with more turns and strengths of string. "The very art and heart of the thing." She clears the table, best she can. Miss Cloris stoops to the box on the floor. When she stands up tall, her arms are full—of collars and shirtsleeves and buttons.

"That's almost every dress she ever wore," Miss Helen says, smiling. "Before she decided against dresses. We had a scissors party. It was . . ." Miss Helen writes into the air with a finger, as if she's tracing the word she'd like to say but can't find the voice for it quite yet.

"Exquisite," Miss Cloris says, finishing the sentence, after a while. She stoops again and straightens again, her arms heavy with more scraps and ribbons and pins and threads. "Now it's your turn," she says, looking at me. "You're in charge."

"In charge?"

"Of the tail of this kite. Make it anything you please."

I stare at Miss Cloris and her pile. I look back toward Miss Helen, who has left the trace of her word in the air.

"It's Joey's birthday coming up, a few months from now," Miss Cloris says. "It's up to you to make the tail right nice."

"The kite's a surprise?"

"It'll be Joey's surprise. We'll drive out to Carter, choose a place on the hill. We'll have him close his eyes until we get the thing flying high. That'll be our job, see? Yours and mine. Miss Helen will keep him occupied, make sure he stays true to the rules."

"That's nice," I say, but suddenly my eyes are hot and everything's swimmy, and where my hunger was my heart is hurting.

"Now, now," Miss Cloris says, leaning toward me, concerned. "What's this about? It'll be a happy day. You'll see."

"I can't go kite flying, Miss Cloris," I say, my breath sucking away.

"We need four for the plan, dear, for Joey's birthday. We'll explain to your mother, if that's your trouble."

"No," I say. "Please! Can't explain it to my mother." I must have shouted a little, because now Harvey's barking and Minxy's on the prowl and Miss Helen and Miss Cloris are looking at me funny, as if they don't know how to turn my crying off, as if this is the actual utmost urgent.

"It won't be for a while yet," Miss Cloris says at last, quieter than I've ever heard her. "An open invitation, if you can swing it. No deciding right now. There's still some time for thinking on it."

"Thank you, Miss Cloris."

"Now, what about the kite tail?"

"Yes, ma'am."

"You still up to that?"

I sniff and nod.

"Any color you want, any texture, any knotting. That is the beauty and the art of the kite tail, like Miss Helen says. It's not *supposed* to be anything, so you can make it all you want." She works through the fabric pile, turns a button with one hand. She pulls a collar from the mess of things. "Remember this?" she asks Miss Helen, and I can tell she's asking for my sake, covering up for my tear burst, making room for me to recover.

"Pure puffery," Miss Helen says, going along with Miss Cloris's plan. "Made you look like a rooster on the prowl."

"And you loved me despite it."

"I loved you always."

They talk like that, back and forth, about the ugly collar and the girly sleeves and the other things Miss Cloris used to wear that now she doesn't, and how it was when they took two pairs of scissors to the old dress pile and chopped the whole thing into scrap pieces. They go on as though I'm not here, as though it's a private place, me at their table, working through a kite tail in my head. I want to say I'm sorry for the shouting. I want to say I'm sorry for not explaining. I want to say, my mother and me, we're out-running the No Good, but I cannot do a thing. I just sit here trying to breathe, and now Minxy comes back

toward my lap and leaps as if my knees are the world's
softest pillow, as if I have been forgiven, as if I can figure it
out—how these scraps make a tail.

By the time Joey comes home, I am recovered and the
kite's in hiding, with its long Rapunzel tail. "Now, that's
making quite a statement," Miss Helen said before Miss
Cloris wheeled her away to the back room.

Miss Cloris cleaned the kitchen of its cotton scraps, hid
the kite somewhere upstairs, came back down and sat with
me, drumming her fingers on the table. Finally she asked if
I knew anything about making sand tarts, and when I shook
my head no, she said, "Never harmed anyone, making two
batches of cookies in a single day." Five things, she told
me, is all that we'd need—the butter, which she'd have to
soften; the vanilla extract, which I found in the pantry; the
confectioners' sugar; which is the snow version of sugar, the
flour, a softer snow than sugar; and pecans, minced down
to nothing. We kept our voices low, and Harvey behaved.
We pressed the sweet dough into star shapes, ate the morning's chocolate chips while we worked. "Forty-five minutes
at two-seventy-five," Miss Cloris told me when the trays
were oven-ready. "Miss Helen likes them brown around
the edges."

We set the timer after that, cleaned up the kitchen.
We talked about anything but kites, anything excepting

Mother, anything at all excluding Miss Helen and her weakness. We each had our hurt spots, I was coming to see, and Miss Cloris was kind, and sometimes she'd say, "Life goes by faster than it ought to," and I'd say, "But sometimes time moves too slow," and either way we weren't judging each other, and when I walked across the kitchen to stare past the alley and around the tree and back on the house where I was living, Miss Cloris didn't ask me for feelings or explaining, only said, "Those crows ought to pay rent, for all the time they spend up on those branches."

I didn't hear Joey until he came through the door, dropped his backpack to the floor, took Harvey's front paws onto his shoulders. "You big old beast," he was saying when I turned around. He smiled his bright white crooked teeth at me. His eyes are on the black side of blue. His hair is like a thousand Slinkys, springing, and his shoulders are built out wide, his body lean. His shorts hung low. He wore no laces in his high-tops. He had a bruise below one knee, fading off to green.

"You're home early," Miss Cloris told him.

"Mr. Shoe took sick."

"Is that right?"

"It is."

"You wash up, now. Miss Helen's waiting."

Harvey whined when Joey set him down, looked like he might jump again. "You never learn, do you, dog?" Joey said, but Harvey yipped like he was sure that Joey would return from around the corner and up the stairs, which, eventually, he did. I followed him to the back room and Miss Cloris followed in time with her plate of browned sand tarts, and we all settled in for the reading—Miss Helen's nothing weight against Joey's shoulder, Minxy on my lap, Miss Cloris beside me. Father Latour was in his adobe room on Christmas Day, humming a song called *Ave Maria Stella.* The sand tarts were disappearing. Joey was stopping every now and then to fix Helen's head on his shoulder. "I'm through at five o'clock," my mother had told me—it felt like a year ago—when she left for work that morning. The clock over the kitchen sink was ticking.

Emmy

Up and up, and then stop, and she's not speaking. We are through again, and down a hall. There is a porch beyond; there is sky—I can almost see sky. "Damn it," she says every time the key sticks, every single time. "Damn it." The bracelet of keys has smudged the knob of Bettina's wrist green. There's the smell of tobacco leaking.

"Where," I ask her for the fourth time now, "are you taking me?"

"To the cleanse," she says for the fourth time. She sounds tired, and still I keep asking. "It's protocol, okay? That's all I can tell you."

She walks and she pushes. She pulls at the hoop in her ear. She won't smile because she can't, and the floor goes bump. She unlocks a door and pushes me through, and now at last we have come to where she has been going. From the white floor, basins rise. The nurses wear white. There is a glassed-in cage of an office, where an owl woman sits, peering through the glasses on her nose.

"Ninth one today," the owl says. "That time of the month." She walks toward me, her hands out in front, her right hand twitching—I see it twitching. I flatten back against my chair.

"Let me do it," Bettina says.

"If that's what you want," the owl answers.

"Do what?" I demand.

"Strip you down," Bettina says—almost a whisper, almost an apology for Dr. Brightman's cure, but she said nothing, absolutely *nothing* when she could have—"for the cleanse." She puts her hands on me, her fingers on the strings of the dress. It takes nothing and I fight her and she says, "The easier you let it be, the easier it is," and I say, "Why? Why? Why?" and she says, "Doctor's orders," and I am naked now, scorching cold flesh, my arm and my leg in their plaster.

"One more into the pot," the owl says over what I say, over what Bettina says back, over the sound of her carrying me now, lifting me and sinking me into a steaming tub, and I am not alone, and I will not look upon the others. "Let the bad leg hang. Wrap the arm."

"Ma'am."

"Cushion for the head. We'll let her steep. Put your hands down, Mrs. Rane," the owl says. "Put your hands down, I warn you." And now Bettina whispers, "Let it be, Emmy. Get it done."

"I am a mother," I say, sobbing.

"Dr. Brightman's orders," she says.

Sophie

We take the long way on the short walk home, stopping at the alley to watch the crows ganging up on the tree, then walking around, to the tree's other side, where no one can see us but us. If you drew a line across the top of my head and kept the line going, you'd come to the shelf of Joey's shoulders. If you looked up, you'd see the one dimple in his one cheek and the thin white scar that goes crosswise across his brow, where the back of the cap usually sits. If you were listening, you'd be listening to the story about the girl at school who left a nest inside her locker and opened it the next day to find birds. "You should have heard those birds," Joey's saying. "You should have seen old Mr. Shoe."

I'm only half listening. I'm watching Joey talk—the lock and unlock of his jaw, the black in the blue of his eyes, the way he looks past me and up into the tree and then looks down again and finds me still here, half listening. "They always talked about it," he's saying now, and I've missed the end of one story and the beginning of the next, and he's caught me and I blush.

"Talked about what?"

"New Mexico. 'Fitting out the Airstream for the South-west,' they'd say."

"Miss Cloris and Miss Helen?"

He looks at me funny.

"Of course them."

"So why didn't they go?"

"Because of me, I guess."

I wait for more of whatever I've missed, whatever he hasn't said yet, but he's stopped. His eyes are drifting away again; his dimple's gone.

"You going to tell me?" I ask him, but his eyes go blacker than blue and his jaw works itself hard and bony silent, and he looks past me for such a long, long time that I wish I could take back my asking.

"Joey?" I ask, and he says, "There were four of us. My parents, my sister, and me. We went out driving to an apple farm. A truck pulled alongside of us and tried to pass but couldn't. I was in the seat behind my mother, in a car seat; I was three. They found me on the roadside, crying."

"Your aunts found you?" I'm so confused. Found him where? What roadside? How did he get there?

"The police. And the police found Miss Cloris, who was my father's stepsister, the only family who could help, or wanted to. Miss Cloris brought me here, and here is home, and I've never known much different. I was three, like I said. My life is here, and most of the time it feels like it always was."

"Oh, Joey," I say.

"It's okay."

"No, Joey, it's not."

"They're good to me—Aunt Cloris, Aunt Helen. They've always done their best."

"What was your sister's name?"

"Jenna."

"How old was she?"

"Six."

"What else do you remember?"

"My mother's hair, which was blowing through the open car window. My father singing some radio song. My sister sleeping. The car was white, with a thin blue stripe, and there were cows in the field where they found me. That's it. That's all I remember."

He stands here, close, and I step closer. I reach for the line across his brow. He lets me touch it, lets me keep my hand near, tells me how Miss Cloris and Miss Helen had been planning an Airstream adventure when the accident happened and he moved in. Cross-country, state by state, their everywhere year—they'd been planning that, and then Joey came. "They put it off," he says, "and kept putting it off, and then my aunt Helen got sick."

"So that's why you read to them, then?"

"I guess that's it."

"To take them to places they haven't been?"

"We pretend."

"You do a nice reading," I say.

I don't ask him what Miss Helen's sick with. I don't ask him for any more talk. I just stand here, on this side of the tree, looking for the blue in his eyes and the dimple in his cheek, tracing the white line across his head. He lifts his hand and tucks my hair behind one ear. He moves closer, and it happens. His lips taste like sugar snow and the fine mince of pecans. I close my eyes and cannot breathe.

"I had to," he whispers when it's over. "Did you mind much?"

"No"—I shake my head—"I didn't."

He leans in again, and this time I kiss him back and the crows above us stir. "It's not fair," I say between kisses, "what happened to you," and he just keeps saying it's all right, until suddenly, from down the road I hear the cough-spit of the Volvo. "Joey," I say, "she's back," and everything changes—Joey and the crows and especially me, pulling away, past the branches toward the street. I run the slate to the door and bang it open. I slam it behind me, tight and sure. "Sophie!" Joey calls, but still I'm running—up the stairs, toward the attic, over the crossbeams, across the pink. I throw the window open and call down to him from there.

"Tomorrow," I tell him. "I promise."

Emmy

❦ ❦ ❦ ❦

Going away, going away, going back, and I am almost home. It was a stream—remember the stream? Emmy, if you can, remember the stream.

"A fighter she is, this Mrs. Rane."

"Soaked me through."

"Me, too."

Mama is pulling an inner tube, pulling me—my bottom wet and my arms spread out, as if my arms are wings. Mama is walking with the water to her knees, the snake of the rope between us making the water striders dance.

Don't move, my love. This is float.

Look at the frogs, eager for sun.

My bathing suit is pink. My bathing suit has a little white belt that I have learned to snap, in and out, like crickets talking.

Emmy, Mama says. *You're growing up.*

Emmy, you are my only.

Emmy, it's just the two of us and the stream.

The sky is leaves. The sky is a lifted sheet of green that won't fall down. The green of peas, the green of grapes, the dark tip green of the beans that Mama snaps between her finger and her thumb. There is a bird making a tree branch heavy, her gray belly bottom like the high back of the sun.

"She's settling now. She won't do harm."

"Jesus. Still morning. When will this day be done?"

To the sea, Mama says. She has her flip-flops on. They are yellow but deep in the muck of the stream. They stir up chimneys of fog wherever they go—piles of white water rising. The soft, pale hairs on Mama's legs glisten where they are wet with steam. In the spaces between my fingers and toes, the dark water runs cool in a backward pull. My bottom's sunk in deep.

I could walk forever, Mama says.

Forever is the sea.

On the banks, the stream runs across the low trunks of the trees. There are shadows beneath the trees and past the trees, and somewhere in the shadows is the chalky path down which Mama and I have come—she carrying the inner tube in the wedge of strength between her arms and ribs, and me in the polka dots of my own flip-flops, the snap and the slap of our feet. *Waiting all winter, all spring for this,* Mama said, and it is still not summer, and sometimes, when the stream bends or the breeze blows, a chill comes in, but in the rubber nest of my inner tube, I snap my belt. The stream is getting bigger now. Stream like a river. It turns over rocks and deeper in my Mama sinks. She hitches her skirt high past her knees and keeps walking.

Close your eyes, says Mama, *and feel the float. Feel the power of the water rising, running.*

There are lilac trumpets on Mama's yellow skirt, and her hem is dark with stream. There are curls at her neck where the hair falls down from the scarf she ties it up with. She hardly bothers with her hair, and even though I am the age I am, I know what it is, who she is: My mama's beauty. Daddy says so, and I think it.

Oh, Lord, Emmy, she says, and she stops.

Mama, what?

Oh, Lord, Emmy. Look there. Must be lost, the poor thing. In the wrong kingdom.

I look to where she points, to the edge of the stream, where, in the rooty banks, a tall bird stands, soft-feathered, its legs like hollow sticks. Mama stops walking, and the tall bird blinks. She says nothing and it shakes its head, cuts the thick air above the creek with the knife of its beak. I float on and on, on the back of the rising, widening stream. I float, and the snake of the rope between Mama and me curves into itself and tangles, and the creek, still getting bigger, carries me forward, on, but still Mama is plunked down like a tree.

Mama! I call, but it's too late, and now I am up against the hard back of her pale thighs with the river of a stream pushing us both to the sea. Mama's knees give. I hear the pop and slide of her yellow flip-flops. *Oh,* she says, a startled sound. *Oh, Emmy,* and her body sways, back and forth, her arms like the limbs of a blown-about tree, until finally she shivers down to her knees. *Oh,* she says, and the big bird digs its head into its neck and rolls back the droop of its wings and lifts high. It lifts and its wings are the sky, and Mama spills into the hurry of the stream—the lilac trumpets on her yellow skirt billowing down.

Oh, Mama says, and she's below me now, tumbled now, the little desperate curls still dry, and I hear another kind of a snap. It's the snake of rope between Mama and me set free. It's me, set free, in the river rising, and the river tightens and deepens; it bends. It's not a stream.

Oh, Emmy. Love.

I turn and see her rising from the muck. I turn and see her reach.

Emmylove.

And the river bends and widens and right at that moment hurries me forward over a table of rocks, and I am sideways to the sea, facing the rooty banks. Behind me, Mama stands and she reaches, but her dress is heavy with the sheen of river and her flip-flop feet are slipping.

You be brave, she calls out after me, and the river writes itself into a new, twisty shape, and when I turn again, there Mama is, swim-running her way to the riverbanks and pulling herself up in the rooty mud with her bare hands, her bare feet; she's lost her flip-flops. Mama is running. She is barefoot through the shadows of the trees, and I am floating and floating with the sizzle of my heart, and the sky overhead is a thin green sheet.

She will run ahead. She will catch me.

Be brave, Emmylove, I am coming.

Mama!

Rescuemerescuemerescueme.

"Oh, good God. Oh, Jesus, Mary, and Joseph, no rest for the weary. Calm yourself, Mrs. Rane."

Mama!

Sophie

❀   ❀   ❀   ❀

"Corned beef," Mother tells me, "and sauerkraut. I got us extra." She's set the two takeouts down and sits while I deal out knives and forks, tear two sheets of paper towels, fold them like napkins. When she pops the lid on her box, the air around us goes sour.

"Still warm," she says. "We're lucky."

She chews and chews. I cut my meat into a thousand pieces. I run my tongue across my lips, tasting the sugar snow of Joey.

"What's the matter?" she asks me, looking up at last, then looking down at my hands—slicing the corned beef into pink stew, into thick soup, into paste.

"Maybe I'm not that hungry."

"And how exactly could that be? You not being hungry?" She lowers her fork and looks at me, suspicious. "It's five fifteen," she says. "Dinnertime. Aren't you always complaining that you're hungry?"

"Bellyache," I lie, quick. "Maybe from the old rice. Shouldn't have made it. You were right."

"You wait this long to tell me?"

"Just started feeling it, a few minutes after five."

"You wait that long to get sick?"

"It just happened."

"Don't disrespect me." She pushes the long parts of her hair over her shoulders. She smoothes the wild eyebrow hairs above one eye. She looks into me like she can see chocolate-chip cookies and sand-tart cookies, Miss Cloris and Miss Helen, Joey and me, the crows in the tree. A twitch starts up in her other eye. "Corned beef not good enough?" she says. "Too big for kraut?"

"That's not it."

"A bellyache?"

"Coming to think of it," I say, "I'm already better." I lift a forkful of kraut to my lips and force it through. I swallow over it and smile. I take a forkful of beef and chew it down, worse than an old eraser. She watches me, takes up her fork, and swallows, suddenly cautious.

"What did you do all day?" she asks now.

"I was reading."

"Reading what?"

"One of those books."

"Which book, Sophie Marks? Be specific or stop lying." Her voice is low and angry, the way it gets before something terrible happens, and if something terrible happens, there will be no stopping it.

"You want to know the truth?" I ask.

"I have been asking you for the truth."

"I was working on my Kepler, making it perfect."

"You were, now?"

"I was."

"I thought you'd finished. Haven't you been saying so—that you finished your Kepler? Haven't you been wanting to read it?"

"Can I be excused, Mother?"

"Excused?"

"To get my Kepler?" My heart is pounding so loud I'm sure she can hear the lie inside it. I'm sure she can see the lie I am. We have to stay here. We can't move—not this time.

"Which is done now?"

"It is. Done and so much better." I fake my hopefulness so hard that maybe suddenly even I believe that I was home all day, refining Kepler.

"You finish your kraut."

"Yes, ma'am."

"You respect your mother."

Emmy

"Emmy, what did they do to you? Where did they take you?"

"Emmy. They do you wrong?"

"Emmy. I'm not leaving you to nothing. You speak to me, you hear me? Unless they cut your tongue?"

"They cut your tongue?"

Someone says it. Someone moans the words.

"There, now," she says. "At least I got you talking."

"You?"

"Me?"

"Leave me alone." My hair is a wet rag. My skin is pickled. My teeth are breaking into chatters. "Please."

Turning my back to her, facing the door. Pulling the sheet up, up over my head, and the air whizzes from the pillow, no case on this pillow, just stuffing and sack. My broke parts stay crooked, like a busted-up letter *K*—the toes inside my cast still pointing to the ceiling. Now the chair wheels are rolling, the flat one going squat. The sheet yanks down. Autumn stares in.

"Hey," she says.

"Can't you let me be?" Can't you? *Can't you?* I want to

scream, and if I scream, they'll do it all again, and I don't scream, and my teeth chatter.

"Tell me what happened."

There's a scar, like a wrinkle, through her lip. There's a gone slash of flesh above one eye. There's a hatching near her chin, the skin too white. "What happened to you?" I ask. I shiver.

"Me? You're the one who got taken."

"I don't want to talk about it. Can't you see? Not talking."

"Was it the cleanse?" She's shifted again, come closer, is stroking a stray strand of hair away from my face. Staring the blue sky of her eyes through me, and something softens, and I nod, and that's all, and the tears riot through, but I do not holler. I do not make a ruckus. I will never make a ruckus again.

"I hate that," she says. "I *hate* the cleanse." Stroking my hair, combing it through, the wet knots and tangles stiffening.

"They've done it to you?"

"'Course they have."

"And you're still here?"

"And bored straight out of my own genius mind." Her lips turn up and the wrinkle vanish-folds. A tear appears in one corner of her eye.

"What's the purpose of it?" I whisper, shivering, pulling the sheet around me hard. "The cleanse, I mean."

"To make us peaceable," she says, but saying it makes her cry. Big tears from both of her eyes, and now she climbs down out of the chair and lies beside me, her forehead to my

forehead, her hand taking my hand. "I remember peaceable,"
she says. "Do you? Think peaceable, Emmy."

"Like the old jigsaw puzzle?"

She almost laughs. "You had one, too?"

"The Peaceable Kingdom," I say. "One thousand pieces."

"'The wolf also shall dwell with the lamb, and the leopard
shall lie down with the kid; and the calf and the young lion
and the fatling together; and a little child shall lead them,'"
she says, and I think of Mama, and I think of our afternoons,
the floppy card table with the foldaway legs, the hundreds and
hundreds of puzzle pieces, and Autumn, younger than me,
puzzle piecing, too—sometime, long ago, who knows how
long, or where, and what secret. I don't think Autumn will
ever tell me her secret. I wait. I wait. Nothing.

"That's some quoting."

"Mrs. Morganton," she says. "Mrs. Morganton taught me."

"Who's that? She work here?"

"Oh, lording Lord, Emmy. No. Mrs. Morganton. Mrs.
Morganton made pies. She made puzzles with me. Before I
got here. When I was free." Autumn puts her fists up to her
eyes and cries. She burbles like a brook. She lies back still.
Past the door is scuffle and howl, the slow and the fast moving. I see it through the window glass, the glass all scratched
with black diamonds.

"Tell me," I say. "Story'll keep us warm. It'll be something."
She slips inside the sheets, touches her forehead to mine, as

if she can give me her thinking that way, thought to thought, no words.

"You ever have a Mrs. Morganton pie?"

"Not as I remember."

"My mother," Autumn says, sniffling now, drying her eyes with the inside arm of her sweater, "she couldn't bake a pie if her life depended on it. But Mrs. Morganton could. Mrs. Morganton pulled the berries from their patch and baked them sweet." The tip of Autumn's nose has gone red, her eyes.

"Tell me about the pies," I say.

"Peaches." Autumn sniffs. "Blueberries."

"Tell me how they tasted."

"Psshhhahh," she says. "There's no describing that."

She pulls her head away and lifts her arm again to blot her nose, and now I see a thin purplish line above the wrist, dug in, but also risen, and I think three years. Three years Autumn's been here, with nowhere to fly and no pies.

"I'll tell you something about my mama," I say. In exchange, I think. Story for story.

"Okay." She sniffs.

"Mama was a hat connoisseur. *Connoisseur*—that's what she said."

"I have never met a connoisseur," Autumn says, and suddenly she's still, still as the glass apple that sits at home beside my box of jewels. What has Peter done with my jewels, or with my mother's rugs, or with her hats—my box of hats?

"Mama was one. She made sensations."

"Sensations," Autumn repeats. In the hall, past the door and the diamond-glass window, people go up and back— toothbrush hair and odd meanders and the guy with the bucket mop, mopping. I feel my heart start thumping again, my shame from the cleanse. "My mother's best hat was white," I say. "A white hat with a brim so wide it fit three of us beneath it—Mama, Father, Emmy. The band on the hat was a mint-green silk. On the knot of the band perched a bird."

"A real bird?" Autumn's eyes gush blue.

"A bird she made with the feathers we found in the path along the river," I say, bringing it back, for her sake, for mine. Bringing Mama back, and her birds. "Gold birds, blue birds, red birds, black," I say. "They'd shiver off their feathers, and we'd find them. All summer long we went hunting for feathers, until Mama had her bird."

"Mmmm," Autumn says, like she's almost sleeping. "A many-feathered bird. A sensation." Autumn lifts her arm and the scar is there. She lowers it, and it disappears.

"Mrs. Morganton lost her husband to the war," she says now. "Said I was the daughter she'd have had if Mr. Morganton was living."

"You should have traded in."

"What?"

"Mothers."

"Ha." She almost laughs. "Should have; you're right. My

mother didn't want me," she says. "I knew from early on. I wanted her to pay."

"Did you?"

"What?"

"Make her pay?"

"She made me pay instead," she says. "She told them I was crazy."

"What happened is your secret, isn't it?" I say.

"Can't speak it," she whispers.

"I'll tell no one," I say.

"It's me," she says, "who can't stand to hear my own story told."

There's noise in the hall, a commotion. There's someone yelling and the elevator ping and Granger on her way and now Autumn turns on her back and moans, throws her bony hand over her eyes. Outside, the wind sneaks up under the loose skirt of the roof tiles, and I pray that somewhere out there Baby is latched in tight. That whoever it is who stole her stole her for love of Baby and not for the harming to Baby, this being my only choice for hoping while I am locked up here—that the thief of Baby thieved for the chance of raising Baby right. That she holds my child close, holds her safe, covers her ears from the wind, until I find her, until I take her home.

"We have to get out of here," Autumn says.

"I know," she says. "We do."

Sophie

❋　　　❋　　　❋　　　❋

In the morning she takes a long time fixing to go. Sits on the edge of her bed, waiting for her Pond's cold cream to settle. Brushes her hair, one hundred strokes around the sagging curves of each ear. Lies back down after the two hundredth stroke, and the air squishes from the pillow and the bed quilt rumples and I stand in the doorway, watching. The soles of her white work shoes are like two faces. Her knees are like hills. Her face is far away; her voice is farther.

"You see what working does," she says after a while.

I nod.

"Can't hear you."

"Ma'am."

"You think I wouldn't have done this life different?"

"'Course you would have."

"I'm playing the lottery, Sophie. Our turn for miracles."

When she's gone, I walk the house considering. Up and down the stairs, through the front room, around the lean of books and the La-Z-Boy, toward the sill, where the salt and pepper shakers from each and every one of Mother's diners are on parade display. Near the shakers, a small pot of plastic geraniums has paled with sun. The only picture on the wall is the old cross-stitch—two bluebirds and words in a scroll: *A Loving Heart Is the Beginning of Kindness.* A thousand *x*'s on a cloth. Four thousand needle pricks. End of the sun like a spilled cup of tea across one corner.

"Our turn for miracles," Mother said, and now I head through the kitchen, past the laundry machines, to the basement door, which is crooked on its hinges. I flip the lights and creak down the planked stairs. There's a tremble of spiderwebs hanging near my head. Pipes crank toward the ceiling, pink rags twisting at the turns. Along the one wall is a long shelf of old paint cans and hard-gleam brushes. Down another is a sawhorse table and little piles of sawdust, left behind the way most everything else down here was left behind by whatever family lived here last. The basement walls are a thick rain color. There's a dirty break of window along one edge, a rag doll twisted on the sill, a hopscotch scotched to the floor.

But it's our boxes that I'm looking for—the ones I carried here on move-in day, marked FRAGILE. The boxes are taped up tight; that's how they travel. They're Mother's personals; that's what she's always said. "Mind your own," she tells me, and I have, moving those boxes house to house and never breaking their seal, never asking. But there are no miracles upstairs, and there are no miracles at the diner, and the only miracle I know for sure starts with setting the No Good free. "Be good," she says, but good is rules I don't understand, and Joey lives next door, and there's a kite waiting to show off its long Rapunzel tail; there's me wanting the kite and wanting Joey.

Mother's personals sit on the shelf above the rusted paint cans. I step-laddered them up. I will step-ladder them down. Tilt the old brown TV box toward me first, because it's the lightest one and the most banged up, the tape loosest at its seams. I'll glue it back maybe—fix it somehow. Mother won't know until we move again. Her knees too bad for basement stairs. Her life too plain exhausting.

You want to know the truth?

I have been asking you for the truth.

It is our turn for miracles.

But it's not miracles I find here, on the basement floor. I find Chief Tankua, Big Jim's Indian friend, instead, still in his Chief Tankua box, his eyebrows bushing out over his eyes. Big Jim is in his own box, too, wearing nothing but crinkly peach-red gym shorts. He can smash a karate board and throw a baseball; that's what the box pictures tell me. He can burst a muscle band by making a fist. He can lie here the way he's been lying here, beside a shoe box of Chevy Camaros and Johnny Lightnings and Plymouth

Superbirds and a Cadillac limo, and there's a house, in Mother's personals, made of dark-blue Legos, and a magazine that's called *The Silver Surfer.* September 18, it says. Fifteen cents. Red crayon and orange crayon scribbling the Silver Surfer.

I find a plastic bat and a Wiffle ball. I find a deck of cards and some cups and spoons. I find a pair of blue-striped sneakers, and a pair of shoelaces, bright orange, in their package. There's a toy telescope and a map of stars and some tiddledywinks and pick-up sticks, and I'm taking each thing out and laying it across the floor—next to and next to and next to—and the spiderwebs float and the sun pushes in, and all I can hear is the pounding of my heart high in my ears, as if my heart is monster size and taking over. It's a store for boys on the basement floor. My mother's personals is boys, her secret. My mother's personals is not a miracle.

The smell is termites, rust, and hopscotch chalk, rain that never dried through. It's crayon wax and the pimples of mold on the back of *Silver Surfer.* One of the Matchbox cars has gotten loose and its front wheel is spinning, and when I park it down, alongside the rest of the miniatures, I hear slide inside the TV box, collapse along the seam lines, and I know that there'll never be any fixing this, any returning the TV box to strictly personal. I have broken a rule, and the proof is here, and I will never be forgiven, and still I am breaking rules and reaching in to the crumble of the old box, laying out what more I find: the yellow sand bucket, the trowel, the stuffed purple turtle, the cake pan shaped like a dinosaur, the plastic bank full of pennies.

Box 1, mother's personals, takes up half the basement floor, gets knocked with window sun. The webs above my head blow like shirts on a line. Still I do not stop—take out and put down, take out and put down—until it's the very last thing in the box: a folded-up newspaper pressed hard across the box's bottom. October 12, 1978, it says. Thursday. A man named Sid Vicious on the front page and a black-and-white fire on page three. TWO TODDLERS KILLED IN THREE-ALARM, the headline says.

Two toddlers killed, both of them boys.

Emmy

A storm is coming. The moon is lying low, out of the way, and the sky is a dirty green-gray bowl. Autumn has pushed me around to the window, which is thick as some old encyclopedia, nailed shut. She lies on her bed with her goggles on, humming some strange little tune.

It's a fortress we're in. It's walls turning on walls, stone into brick, castle tops and concrete roofs, stairs on the outside spiraling toward inside, a flat pan of lawn. The courtyard is spoked with concrete pathways, and at the far corner, through the open arch, lies the long skinny road—Carter Road, Autumn called it. On the one side of the road, she says, lie the nurses' quarters. On the other lies a long, wide field—used to be corn there, Autumn says, and cows, back when State grew its own food. You can't see the road or the fields or the houses from here, but Autumn's been through it all, three times and again—my orientation, she says, to State. "Dietary," Autumn has said to me, standing near, pointing to the parts of State we can see. "Laundry. Mending. Warehouse. Print Shop. Photo Lab. X-ray. Commissary. Office." A madness of doorways and panes, arches and bridges, all of it connected, Autumn has promised, by bridges and walkways, secret tunnels.

"Where's the infirmary?" I asked her.

"There," she said, pointing across the lawn, where the light through the windows was yellow-green and the windows were cut high, into ribbons.

"A month," I said.

"A month you been there?"

"A month," I said, and I started to cry. Autumn bent near and threw her toothpick arms around me, but already my teeth had started to chatter, and the skinniness of her couldn't get me warm, and when I couldn't stop, she whispered, "You better tell me. You better, Emmy," until finally I said, "They took my Baby," and she pulled back, and she stood tall, her eyes so wide.

"I will kill them," she said, like she already knew all the wrong the world can do and like she had powers against it, like she had guessed me to be a mother all along.

"I just want her back," I said, "is all."

"So we will get her."

"Can't get her stuck in here."

"Of course we can't."

"She's out there," I sobbed—pointed past the courtyard, the mean spokes, through the archway, down the road, past the fields, toward the highway. "Out there, and I can't reach her."

"Bastards," she said. "One and all."

She leaped, furious, like a dancer, to her bed. She began to hop, the mattress rasping and squeaking beneath her and the room shaking. "I do my best thinking up here," she explained, not even a little out of breath, touching her toes when she jumped now, kicking her feet, grabbing at the back of her heels, jumping at a terrible speed, her brow wrinkled, her eyes glazed, her hair slapping her shoulders.

"You some kind of gymnast?" I said at last, my sobbing gone over to surprise. She was wearing a green dress and purple stockings, big hole in one toe.

"A genius," she said. "Didn't I tell you?"

"You coming up with a plan?"

"I'm getting my mind ready," she said, "for the planning."

She made one final huge pounce, down and up, her head practically scraping the ceiling tiles. She folded midair and collapsed, her back slapping against the rumpled sheets of her bed, the mattress still rasping beneath her. She closed her eyes, then leaped up suddenly again, stole her goggles from the globe, pulled them on, over her head, and returned to the bed, her face squished, her eyes at a great distance. "Almost forgot," she said, and started humming her strange little tune.

I stayed in my chair at the window, watching her mind wheels spin, until it was as if she had gone into some magician's trance, into a place that was hers and was private, and so I turned to watch the window again, to watch the lights going on, the doctors straggling through, the nurses, the patients, leading away and out, toward my baby. I remembered the plume of the plane, and the ants, and the green. I remembered the sock, so yellow and lacy. I remembered Peter when he came to me in the room the police took me to: "Your hair is a mess," he said. "You're filthy dirty." There was the white strip of skin where his wedding band had been. His hair was toughed-up bristles. His gray T-shirt was tucked into his stiff blue jeans, and his shirt was undone at the neck.

"Tell them I'm not crazy," I begged him. "Tell them that."

"I'm not lying," he spit, "for your sake."

A wind rasps at the window. I rake my hair through. I pull the thin smock close, but it does no good, and now I remember Mama, the last year she was sick, the smell in that room, the shadows. The bureau on the back wall. The chest on the floor. The bedpan, shaped like a horseshoe. The coil of the rug, which was the color of the quilt, the mirror, the tin of buttons, the shoe box of feathers. I'd bring her applesauce, still warm in the bowl. I'd make it for her, alone in the kitchen——the naked fruits the color of bone, the fire high beneath the pot, the pulp that I would strain through and through, cut a Bartlett into it, a squeeze of lemon, a shake of cinnamon. "I made you applesauce," I'd say, and she'd say, could barely say, "Emmy, you are my only."

Mama died, and Daddy went heartbroke, and heartbreak kills you just as sure as cancer does, and I didn't have choices, and there was Peter, and there is Baby out there waiting.

"What are we going to do, Autumn?" I ask. "What is there for us?" But before I can hope for an answer, there is a knock on the door, a key in the lock, Bettina with her cups and her pills.

"How are you getting on?" she asks, and Autumn starts humming louder.

Mama made puppets out of Daddy's socks and painted cotton balls. She built Christmas wreathes out of old pinecones. She was a pipe-cleaner artist. Made pipe-cleaner tigers. Made lions and deer and ocelots. Bent the pipe cleaners and fluffed them up, and later I'd find them prowling toward me in the trees or sleeping in the flower beds or clinging to the fence that divided our lawn from Mr. Jenkins's. Mama could do most anything. Mama would have rescued me.

She'd have known to find me here.

She'd have rescued Autumn, too.

We'd have been sisters.

Part Three

Sophie

❀   ❀   ❀   ❀

"Shhh, now," Miss Cloris is saying. "You take your time. Miss Helen and I aren't going anywhere, and Harvey's about to behave. Like a good pup, Harvey is."

"I'm sorry," I try to say. "I'm sorry." But the tears keep pouring out, and Minxy stays put on the windowsill, and Miss Helen reaches for my hand, smoothes my fingers down with hers, and I can't stop crying. "I shouldn't have busted in," I sob, trying to press my other hand to my face to stop the tears, but the tears have a mind of their own.

"You don't be silly. Our door is open."

"I just couldn't . . . ," I start, and now I really can't go on, and Miss Cloris pushes up from the front-room couch, where she's been sitting on the other side of me, and goes halfway to the kitchen, then stops and turns back, unde-cided.

"You bring us something to read, Sophie?" she asks at last. "Is that it?" She means the page three I yanked from the basement when I started running—up the rattle of planks, beneath the trembling web, past the Maytags, through the kitchen, out the front door, which slammed hard behind me, and kept on slamming, as I ran the slate, past the acorn splat, to the walk, and up the steps to the Rudds'. I knocked but I didn't wait for any answer. I pulled the knob and stumbled in, and in the very first room, I found them, Miss Helen and Miss Cloris, holding hands. They made room for me between the two of them, and I haven't moved since, even though Harvey is banging his fat tail hard on the bright wood floor, wanting up and in between us, and Minxy on the sill seems eager to jump, and Miss Cloris still cannot decide if a drink or sweets can fix this.

"A house fire," she says now, lifting the headlines from my lap, where I had left them. "October 1978," she reads to Miss Helen. "Two toddler boys the victims."

"That is indeed a sad story," Miss Helen says, "I can see why it caused you a commotion."

"That's not it." I can hardly get the words out.

"That's not it?" Miss Cloris asks. Through my flooding eyes I see the mix-up in Miss Cloris's face—her wanting to be kind, but her confusion.

"I mean that's not the only it. The fire is it, but the boys—they're my brothers." I burst with the words, like a big exploding hydrant.

"I'm afraid I don't understand," Miss Cloris says, tucking in beside me, unfolding the whole page three so she can read beneath the picture of the two-story house in the pretty neighborhood going up in flames and smoke. "'I thought they were outside,' Mrs. Cheryl Marks, twenty-five, is reported to have said," Miss Cloris reads to herself but also to Miss Helen. "'I thought they were playing on the swing.'" She reads on—about the boys and their ages, the boys and their father, away on business when the fire happened. She reads about Cheryl Marks, a librarian at the local library, who was in her bedroom working her Singer sewing machine when the fire happened. She thought the boys were outside. She threw up the sash and jumped. Sailed from the second-floor window into a low row of hedges, leaving it to a neighbor to carry her off and leaving it to the police to sadly inform her that her boys had been playing inside. They had been trapped and she'd gotten out. The source of the fire remaining under investigation.

Miss Cloris presses her knee into my thigh and cups my chin in the big softness of her hand.

"Sophie," she says, "you look at me. This was 1978. Those boys were four and five."

"I know what it said. I can read."

"Honey, this is 2004, and you're—you're how old now?"

"Fourteen."

"That makes you born in 1990, Sophie. Your brothers would be in their thirties by now."

"But Cheryl Marks is my mother. And those boys were my brothers, because they were in my mother's personals."

"I'm afraid I don't understand, love."

"In the basement."

"You found this in the basement?"

"With their toys and things, in a box. I was looking for a miracle. . . ."

"In the basement, love?"

I nod. "In a box. And that's what I found. My brothers' toys. My mother's story."

I feel Miss Helen's hand press down harder on mine and Miss Cloris's knee unjab my thigh. I hear Minxy fly from the windowsill and paw her way into my lap. Miss Cloris makes a big, sad sigh, then takes my free hand up in hers, and now I have no hands with which to wipe my tears, and they pour down my cheeks, my chin, my neck. My T-shirt's soaking.

"Nothing's impossible," Miss Cloris says. "Of course it's not."

"Because it explains everything," I say.

"Everything?" Miss Helen asks.

I nod, and then the tears come hard again.

"Why don't you tell us," Miss Cloris says, "just what you mean."

Emmy

❀   ❀   ❀   ❀

Bettina says, "If I see one ounce of trouble, one trembling inch, you will be reported, privileges revoked."

"Yes, ma'am." Autumn nods.

"No wild shenanigans."

"None."

"No bumper cars with the nurses' stations."

"We swear."

"No giving other patients rides for the cheap thrill of it. Not every patient who needs a wheelchair gets a wheelchair. Make proper use."

It's the same every day, after we wait in line with the others for the shower and lavatory, after Bettina helps me in and out of my chair, after breakfast, which is potatoes, runny or mashed. After Talk Therapy, Music Therapy, Crafts Therapy, Autumn's in charge, and Autumn has stories—one for every inmate, one for every day that she's been here.

"That's Wolfie," she'll tell me. "Thinks she's Hollywood. Get a good look at her hair."

"That's Jeannie in the Bottle."

"Why?"

"It's her face," she says. "The way it's smooshed." Autumn pushes me slow so I can see for myself. She whistles above me, so that we won't be suspect.

"You meet Virgin Mary yet?"

"How could I?"

"Virgin Mary and her diet of petals. Flower petals. Best friends with Liesel the dancer. Liesel hears music everywhere."

They unbandaged my arm, took away the sling. They left me with a scar that runs like a track from the hill of my shoulder to my wrist. Autumn said to be proud of the scar. Called it my survivor tattoo. Runs her finger down its ridge, but all this time, all this talk, how many days, she won't give up her secret. She wheels me floor to floor, down the halls, past the benches, whistling. She calls out to Julius, the mop man, to shine the floors.

"You're all the shine this place needs," Julius will tell her, and she'll whistle at him, laugh like she's honking through a horn. "Too bad he's four hundred years old," she'll whisper down into my ear, and I'll wonder how Autumn will ever break out of here, how she'll break me free, how we'll find Baby. It's like she's part of them now, like she belongs to this place, like no one can know it the way she does, like she has no choice, except that every single day Autumn is scheming. "Today we're flying free," she'll say. "We're keeping our minds clear," she warns me. We spit out our pills soon as Bettina's back is turned—slide them through the slot in the side of Autumn's globe; it's a bank globe. "Bettina's in love with Dr. Brightman," she'll tell me, when the blonde one with the ruler smile is gone. "She was born here," she'll tell me. "'Cause her mother's crazy."

"That true?" I'll ask her.

"Ask her if you want," she'll say, and then her eyes will go so wide that I can't tell if she's lying.

Down the hall she takes us. Past the benches, past Wolfie, wearing her Marilyn Monroe hair, past Jeannie, pressing her face against the window, past Liesel, who wears pink slips and jazz hands and a fake moonstone on her wedding-band finger, past Fanny, who was Autumn's roommate once, before Fanny got too crazy. "Roomie number five," Autumn says whenever we pass her by, and I don't know if Fanny is her real name or just the nickname Autumn calls her, but her smock splits open in the back and she doesn't mind, she has no shame, and Autumn says Fanny's in love with Cavity, who only has two teeth in his head.

The hall bends into a high bang of traffic and carts, women with brooms, men with cigarettes, ash eyes and skin. "Hey, Wolfie," Autumn will say, and Wolfie will puff up her hair, like this is a movie we're in. At the elevator, we'll wait for the ping. When the ping pings, we'll go two floors down, and when the doors open, we're flying—breeze in my hair, tile loose beneath the wheels, the bad wheel in a dull squeal—and now we're past the library, past the office, past a long bank of windows, and this, the windows, is where we stop to watch the world going by. Autumn stands beside me in an angel stream of sun, and she is young, her arms so skinny. She'll kiss the part in my hair with her chapped pair of lips, and little by little, she'll stop whistling, and always, always, she'll wink at the guard in his chair, who sits at the desk that stands between the inside and the outside, the door that leads to the courtyard. "I've got him under my spell," she'll tell me.

"I want to ask you something," she says now, her breath in my hair, the *s*'s skipping across my scalp.

"What something?"

"Do you believe in people?"

"People, Autumn?"

"People."

"I do. Some people."

"Then tell me a story?" She reaches for my hand and squeezes it tight, as if she won't breathe again until I start talking.

"First night of Baby's living, she took my hand," I say.

"Took your hand? For real? With her baby fingers?"

"Took them, squeezed them," I say, because it's true. "Let me know that she was real."

"Oh," she says, the smallest word, and she doesn't whistle; she doesn't dance, or even move. She stands there beside me, watching the world beyond the glass, the patients with walking privileges walking the spokes of the courtyard, the birds in the one tree, the row of azaleas, their flowers gone, their branches stiffened.

"What's our plan?" I ask her after time goes by.

"Thinking of flying," she says, as she always says. "Only way," she tells me, "of getting free. We have to be free to find Baby. Have to get up some speed and fly."

"We do," I say. "I know."

"Look," she says, pointing across the courtyard to the tree, where crows are squatting. "Do you see them?"

"I do."

"Those are some wings," she says. "Nice and sturdy."

Sophie

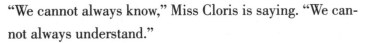

"We cannot always know," Miss Cloris is saying. "We cannot always understand."

"Though sometimes we do," Miss Helen says, barely a whisper. She puts her hand on Minxy, still curled in my lap, and Miss Cloris reaches for it. They stay like that, hand in hand over me, until Minxy turns and knocks a paw to Miss Helen's smallest finger.

The sun is in a different place. Harvey's asleep. Miss Cloris has come and gone and come with a plate of cheese and a Bartlett pear, cut into quarters. She's poured from the pitcher of pink lemonade, until there's nothing left but ice cubes and seeds. I've told my story the best that I can—our running from the No Good, the promises I break, the rules I don't abide more and more often. I've told them that there is one box more of my mother's personals, and that after this, when I go home, I'm going to break the tape, unlock the secrets.

"Maybe we should come with you," Miss Cloris said, and I said, "So long as I know you are right here, I'm fine."

"Sometimes it's better to take the news slowly," Miss Helen cautioned.

"There's truth," I said, "and I want it."

"Maybe we should invite your mother for a visit, treat her to some courtesies, let her talk."

"I need some time," I said, "without her suspecting."

Miss Cloris stands and starts pacing. Harvey shakes himself awake and trots to the door. "You stay in the side yard," Miss Cloris tells him, opening the screen to let him through. Then she walks in little circles around the room, pushing at the hair on her head.

"I don't like this," Miss Cloris says. "Not one bit. The two boys and the No Good and the hiding—and you, Sophie, living as you have, one of the brightest girls I've ever met, sneaking your way into the sun."

"Childhood should be an adventure," Miss Helen says. "All of living should."

"So much inside air," Miss Cloris says. "It breaks my heart."

"Though here you are," Miss Helen says. "That counts for something."

"Illegally," Miss Cloris says, "at least according to her mother."

She keeps walking and pushing at her hair. Minxy rolls and makes the leap to the bright floor. Miss Helen leans against my shoulder, and in the yard, Harvey whines for someone to play. It must be one o'clock by now, or two, my mother working toward the end of her shift, playing her Lotto, wanting her miracle, and maybe her miracle isn't money after all, but the undying of two boys in a fire, the unsmashing of knees, the unlying to me, over all these years. My mother's personals is truth by way of lies. It's the lockup of her, and the gaps in between, and it's the No Good and my father, Andrew Marks, in the bottom of a box, in a story: away on business. And when he came home, what? And when I was born—what then?

"Miss Helen," I ask, "you okay?" She straightens her head and shifts her weight, and Miss Cloris comes to help her—fits one hand to Miss Helen's face and another to her shoulder until she is sitting up on the couch inside her own balance, her wheeled chair catching the sun spokes in the corner.

"You leaving, child?"

"Yes, ma'am."

"And returning?"

"I will."

"You call. You holler. You don't knock. You understand?"

"Ma'am?"

"Yes?"

"Tell Joey I say hi?"

"Of course."

"Tell him I'm glad he ended up living here with you."

"Tragedy and blessing," Miss Cloris says. "Sometimes they're the same one thing."

Emmy

"You were warned," Bettina says, and she says it so sadly. "You were trusted."

"Yes, ma'am," Autumn says, and I echo, "Yes, ma'am, yes."

"I asked for calm and not commotion."

"It was an accident."

"I asked for civility, respect."

"We weren't meaning disrespecting."

"Weren't meaning doesn't matter, Autumn. You start running like you did, and this whole place goes to chaos, and now Cavity's in the infirmary—sliced deep and clean right here." Bettina draws a line above her eye to mark the spot where the skin split after Cavity got to running behind our wheelchair brigade and smacked the floor with his face. Cavity tripped. Cavity's in the infirmary. Autumn kept running; we were flying. "Getting sewn up in the blood zone," Bettina continues. "Which is your doing." We sit in a small room with a closed door, Bettina's legs crossed at the ankles, her fingers pulling at the wooden cross that she wears around her neck. My heart is a frog in my chest.

"It wasn't my fault," Autumn says, "what Cavity did. Cavity

is Cavity." Her hands make somersaults across her lap. She swings her feet above the linoleum floor.

"Do you know what inciting is, Autumn?"

"We were just getting up our speed. We didn't mean harm."

"This is a *hospital*, Autumn. There is no speed." She drops the cross and ties up her arms beneath her chest, sighs heavy. She leans back against the lawn-colored chair. There are vertical seams above her nose, between her eyes. There's a rash of red up high on one cheek. She smells like coffee, paste, cigarettes, old ammonia. There's commotion in the hall beyond us, a rectangle of light that comes through the window in the door.

"Do you want to explain?"

Autumn shakes her head no.

"I need to know, Autumn, what the speed was for."

Autumn's head swings, side to side. "Can't tell. That is our secret."

"You need to be straight with me, Autumn."

"Secrets are secrets."

"You had my trust, Autumn. You had privileges."

Had, she is saying. Had. Had.

"It was the crows' fault," Autumn says at last.

"I don't see how crows could have anything to do with this, Autumn."

"Because they were flying."

"You need to tell the truth."

"That is the truth. They were flying, and we wanted to fly, too."

Bettina looks from Autumn to me and back again. The ruler of her mouth won't bend.

"We didn't mean to hurt anybody," Autumn says, pleading. "We're sorry for Cavity."

"The facts are the facts, Autumn. Always."

"We were just practicing."

"Practicing?"

"Stretching our wings."

"Ma'am," I say, but Bettina barely glances my way, and Autumn won't look at me either, as if to look at me is to make a suspect of me, as if it were not my fault that we were flying in the first place, practicing our speed, for Baby's sake, for going free.

"We meant no harm," Autumn says, her lips thin as a fly's wing, bitten into and raw.

"Meaning and doing harm are two separate things, Autumn."

"Please," Autumn says. "It won't happen again." Something in her blue eyes cracks. Something splits and spills, and in this moment I understand that Autumn is the only thing I have. The only sure and actual. I want to reach for the fumbling hands on her lap. I want to hold them, each one, and keep them safe from whatever is going to happen next.

"It's my fault," I say. "I made her do it."

"You made Autumn race you down the hall in your wheel-chair?" Bettina asks, very quietly, very slow.

"Yes, ma'am."

"You made her swerve and tilt? You made her holler?"

"I didn't hear her holler."

"You put Cavity in the infirmary?"

"It was me," I say, "and I apologize." I won't look at Autumn, because I know she will beseech me. I won't look into her blue eyes leaking. I look hard and steadfast toward Bettina. I say the words as if it's trial and jury, defendant and witness. As if it's seven weeks ago, or eight, or however long since Peter sat there saying I was crazy.

Bettina looks from Autumn to me and back again. She pushes her heels into the floor, stands up, pulls at the cross on her neck, sighs, and now her mouth bends, but it bends downward. She rubs at the rash near her eye. "I need to talk to Nurse Granger," she says finally. "You two wait here."

She walks to the door and locks it behind her. She stares in at us through the glass in the door and then she walks away.

"Psshhhahh," Autumn says, scrubbing at her eyes with the balls of her fists. Her arms are so skinny, it's like they're only made of bone, like skin is the sleeves that Autumn puts on.

"What will she do?" I ask. "What happens next?"

She shrugs and a tear breaks from her eye. "This is State,"

she says, shuddering, and I want to reach for her, climb out of these wheels, escape with her to somewhere safe, but the door is shut and Bettina's key has turned the lock. Whatever it is has been done, and Cavity's lying in the infirmary, a line of blood above one eye.

Sophie

❉　　　❉　　　❉　　　❉

The Volvo coughs to a stop and I'm ready—the kitchen clean and the La-Z-Boy polished, a long glass of ice water sitting still among the towered books, which I have rearranged according to their sizes.

"Have a seat," I say when Mother drags in. "Put your feet up." I ease the take-homes from her hands, trade them for Ziplocs of ice for her smashed-in knees. I do not look into her eyes, because if I look into her eyes, she will see that I am lying. That in the basement beneath us her personals are scattered. That in the house next door, they know her story. I have broken her first rule: Be good.

"You play the Lotto?" I ask her, taking the leftovers into the kitchen, slipping them into the cool of the refrigerator, coming back.

"No miracles," she says.

"Maybe tomorrow?"

"Taking tomorrow off."

"You are?" I ask, stopping cold in my tracks.

"Marge wants a double shift. Told her she could have

mine. Need my rest, Sophie. That's the truth. Need time at home with you."

I nod. Say nothing. Don't look anywhere near her so she can't see into my heart.

"Now, what's all this for?"

"What do you mean?"

"The niceness of things. The ice water."

"Just want you comfortable," I say. "After your long day."

"You sure that's all?" She looks at me up and down and my stomach goes wormy.

"I'm sure."

"You don't sound so sure." She studies me harder, then settles into her chair. Slips out of her white shoes and pulls at the strands of her hair. One of the hairs gets loose and curls free and floats slow to the floor, and now she closes her eyes and lifts the long glass of water to her lips.

"Well?" she says.

"Well?"

"Come and join me."

I sit opposite her in the cranky old rocker. I creak back and forth, watching the sun heating her Ziploc knees, the ice melt to nothing. "You ready to hear my Kepler?" I ask before she can ask me about my day.

"I suppose I am."

"'From Nothing to Big Things,'" I say, my voice suddenly shaking. I cough, pretend it's a tickle. I lift the paper from the floor, where I'd slipped it an hour ago, for this purpose. I start at my beginning: "'Johannes Kepler was born with the skies in his eyes. He was born looking up so he could see.'" I glance up to find that Mother's eyes are closed. The line between her brows is deep.

"I'm listening."

"All right."

"'The skies in his eyes,'" she repeats.

"I thought . . ."

"Keep reading."

I steady my voice over every word and phrase.

We eat dinner in the same chairs, the take-homes in plates on our knees. For a long time, she doesn't talk, just chews.

"So you've befriended Mr. Kepler," she says at last.

"I liked his story." I smothered my hot dog with the yellow mustard we keep inside the refrigerator door. It still tastes like water that has boiled many things. When I chew, it slides around in my mouth.

"'Skies in his eyes,'" she repeats. "'Born looking up.' 'A heart shattered but still beating.' You know he had a broken heart, Sophie? For a fact? It said so in the books?"

"I just assumed."

"But why assume?"

"Because look at him, Mother. Look at his life. His father going away and not returning. His children dying, and then his wife. His mother put on trial for witchcraft. His own country locking him out."

"Johannes Kepler was the father of celestial mechanics," Mother says. "His mathematics explained the shapes of honeycombs. He created the science of optics. He revolutionized the study of solids. And here you come, with your Kepler essay, talking about sadness and heartbreak."

"I wanted to tell his story. His real story."

"That's not what you've done. You've written fiction. Your ideas about how a man feels. A man you've only met in books."

"How else would I meet him?"

"You know what I mean."

"How else would I meet *anyone*?"

She stares at me or through me, her eyes dark coals, her eyes full of all she's never told me. Bobby and James. Four and five. A fire. She left them. She jumped. Her smashed-in knees are not her work-ruined knees. Her smashed-in knees are burning. Why does she keep their things in a box, and why can I not ask her, and why has she hidden the truth all these years, and where is my father, and why are we still running? What proof does she have that the No Good wants us? That we aren't our own strange version of already free?

"What do you suppose Kepler wished to be remembered for?" she asks me now. "What do you suppose any of us,

Sophie, wish to be remembered for? For the things that tried to stop us or the ways we carried on? Think about that, Sophie, next time you choose to write an almost version of a man."

"Yes, Mother," I say, my voice all smoke and anger.

"Don't speak to me that way."

"What way?"

She lets her head fall back against the La-Z-Boy. Another loose hair floats to the floor. She stares beyond me, toward the sill of salt and pepper shakers, the thousand silky *x*'s: *A loving heart . . .*

"Does that dog ever stop barking?" she asks after a while.

"Harvey's a good dog," I say.

"Is that a fact?"

"It is." I stand, leave my mustard-smeary hot dog plate right on the chair, where I know I shouldn't. I cut straight past her, walk the loud heart of the stairs, slam the door to my room.

"Don't you slam that door, Sophie Marks," I hear her calling from below.

I open the door. I slam it harder.

Emmy

Autumn isn't to leave. She is to stay right here, Room 433, Cot B, watching the world through the window, except when Bettina comes and takes her down the hall to the shower and stalls, then brings her back, walks her inside, locks the door.

"I will die," she said when Bettina told her, and all that night I held her in my arms, and nothing that I said could stop her from shaking. "I'll never get out," she kept saying. "Never get free." A wind blew in, lifting the ever-loosening tiles on the roof above our heads. Clouds heavied in, then slipped away, like a curtain drawn back over the moon.

"Bright out," I said. But Autumn wouldn't look up to see.

They bring her breakfast, lunch, and dinner on cardboard cafeteria trays—runny potatoes with bacon on the side, a slab of Spam, a bowl of peaches, celery sticks smoothed over with peanut butter. They turn the lock. Sometimes somebody from Services will come, pull the curtain down the center of the room, and talk quiet and firm, and Autumn will lie there with her goggles on, humming some tune, hardly listening.

"You have to behave," I'll tell her afterward.

"I have to get out," she'll say. She wears three sweaters, a yellow tube top, a pair of leggings, bare feet. She wears her red circus skirt and a gray sweatshirt. She wraps her neck with a bright red scarf and calls herself the Red Baron. She studies the globe, rattles the pills that we've fed it. She points to countries, cities, mountains, seas. "Baby's out there," she says. "We have to find her."

"Seven months," I say.

"Seven months what?"

"Baby's seven-month birthday, or thereabouts."

"You think she's talking by now?"

"Don't think so."

"You think she's still in this country?"

"Better be."

"You think the guy with the bike is still out there looking?"

"Arlen?" I ask. "Arlen, you mean?"

"Funny name for a guy," she says.

"Funny person." Though when I think of Arlen now, I think of what he did for me. Of how he said to hold on, hold on. I think of Mama lying in her bed at the end, my hand in hers, her hand slipping. "I raised a good daughter," she said, and that was the last thing she said, the very last of Mama's words.

They cut the cast from my leg; my leg's white and skinny. They gave me lessons in walking again. "Go at your own pace," they tell me, and I have taken it slow, leaving Autumn only when they make me, when they force me to go up and down the long tunnels of the halls, over the bridges, past the bay of windows, past the guard, to Music, to Crafts, to Dining, to Talk. It is crowded at State. I'm on my own.

The library is hush, a room with a view. It is Miss Cilla Banks, three hundred years old, who has plopped herself down in a big chair to read, and who doesn't mind me, so long as I don't disturb her reading.

"You understand the Dewey decimals?" she asked me the first day I opened the door and pushed through, and I told her yes, I know Mr. Dewey. Mama was the one who made our acquaintance, who took me to the library Saturday mornings and said, "Pick out a book for yourself." I asked Mama once what the spine numbers mean. "Branches of knowledge," she said, explaining how every book has a second name that gets chalked down low on the spine. We went up and down the stacks, Mama and me. We found big words. We wrote them down. We made up songs to sing. When we got home, we worked the kitchen together—Mama rubbing my father's steak and me snapping the tips off of beans.

Miss Banks wears a navy housedress like the kind no one but the cat is supposed to see. The dress has big white buttons down the front and a single brown one, except sometimes a white circle button goes missing and sometimes it's replaced with a fat red square as if rearranging buttons is Miss Banks's method of accessorizing.

"Coming to read?" Miss Banks will ask when I walk in,

never looking up to see whether I nod yes or shake my head no, and not minding where I go, which stacks I walk to, which book I take down to the floor and read. It can go for an hour like that, just the two of us—Miss Banks the librarian in her stuffy chair and me on the floor, and sometimes Julius will come in, leave his mop and bucket at the door, and spend ten minutes or more with the *Daily News*. Or sometimes a doctor will come by, or a nurse, and when that happens, Miss Banks will lift the glasses from the chain around her neck and pinch them up to her nose and ask, "Subject matter? Title? Author?" in that order, and whoever has come has to answer so that Miss Banks can point them to where they should go. They sign their name on a clipboard pad when they take a book from the room. They toss it back into a bin when they are done.

I find the books that Mama read to me. I take them back to Autumn, to read to her at night. I crawl in beside her on her cot and she watches the moon, and I read, and when I'm done, she'll ask me if I have ever had a garden of my own, or if I ever met a thief kind as Ali Baba. She'll smile, but it's not like the smile of before, and she doesn't wear her goggles anymore, and for three days straight she hasn't changed her leggings. "Psshhhahh," she says, when I tell her good night. She touches her finger to her heart and turns.

"I can't take it," she says. "I can't take it anymore." And every time a black crow caws, she sobs into her pillow.

Sophie

Clouds have come in; the sky is dark. Miss Cloris and Miss
Helen go back and forth on the porch swing, the loose bits
of chain snapping against the long links whenever the chair
rocks back to its center. I can hear their voices rising—the
sound of their words, but not the words themselves. I watch
the windows in their house for Joey passing. At last the
screen door slams and Harvey's down there barking, and
when the door slams a second time, it's Joey in the alley,
play-wrestling that dog to the ground. The only light there is
is the leak of light that falls from the porch toward the alley.

"You'll get the police called," Joey's warning Harvey,
"if you don't stop your yipping." But Harvey keeps on singing to the hidden moon, and Joey wrestles him harder, tries
to shush him. On the front porch, the swing chains come
to silence and Miss Cloris stands to scoop Miss Helen into
her arms. I see their half-shadows on the porch boards.
I hear their whispers rising. Now the door slams and there's
nothing, then there's Cloris flipping on the kitchen lights.
I watch her lower Miss Helen into a kitchen chair and then
walk toward the sink, where I can't see her.

"Joey," I whisper-call through the tree limbs. Against the kitchen light, he's a silhouette, and Harvey's all for action, jumping his paws to Joey's shoulders. Joey takes the dog's weight, then presses down on his cap and fits his hand over his eyes. "Hey," he says at last, when he finds me staring through the night. "You okay up there?"

"I don't know," I say. "You okay?"

He shakes his head. "Wish I could see you. For real, I mean."

"Wish it, too."

Harvey whines and noses up to Joey's chin. Joey laughs, takes Harvey's front paws, and holds him still, like the start of a dance.

"You sure you can't come out?" Joey asks me.

"I am."

"Your mother awake?"

"She's left the door to her bedroom open. She'd hear me on the stairs."

"It's a good night," he says. "Even moonless."

"I know."

"Got all my homework done."

"That's nice."

"Have an idea," he says finally, lowering Harvey to the ground.

"What's that?"

"Just don't go anywhere. That's all I'm asking."

"I'm not going anywhere, Joey Rudd."

He reaches into Harvey's collar, drags him around to the front porch and up through the door; I watch it all in silhouette. Then the door slams again, and Joey's back outside, a dark shadow with a backwards cap making its way to the base of the oak. I hear leaves rubbing leaves and the snap of a twig. I hear the croak of a limb yanking downward.

"What are you doing?" I whisper through the knots of the tree.

"Rapunzel, Rapunzel," he says, "let down your golden hair."

I see the tree shiver in the dark. I hear sneakers slip against the bark, then hold. Farther up, nearer to me, the leaves turn into wings and the wings are the night crows flying free, and the wings are in me, too—the way my heart turns over on itself, the way my stomach flutters.

"You're going to hurt yourself," I warn him.

"Am not."

"Watch out, will you?" My words are breath.

"I'm watching."

"Can't see you."

"There's a distance," he says, "and I'm climbing."

It's shadows and gray, the crooked lid of his cap. It's the arms of the tree, its elbows twisted, its leaves shaking loose to the ground. High up, near me, the tree starts shuddering harder, and Joey cries out, and now there's silence and the tree goes much too still.

"Joey?" I ask, my heart in my throat.

"It's nothing," Joey says, his voice straining.

"Some night for no moon," I tell him, and now I can't swallow, and I don't want him to stop, but he has to, because what if he falls, and what if he's hurt, and what if it's my fault, because it would be?

"Tree's a dream," he grunts, "for climbing," and all of a sudden the tree's alive again, as if someone picked it up to shake it. I hear the grab of Joey's hands among the leaves, the splitting of the bark beneath his shoes, the falling away of cracked twigs. Finally I see his fist punch through the tree shadows, and then his wrist, and then his shoulder, and then his head. I smell chocolate chips and dog kiss, the leather belt that slaps long at his waist. I watch him riding that limb as if he's riding some horse and pray that my mother's still sleeping.

"I didn't know you could do that," I whisper.

"Trees are meant for climbing."

"You be careful."

"Am being." Across the alley, a light snaps on in the upper hallway, and I can see more of Joey now, see the knobs of his hands, the leaves in his hair, the tear in his T-shirt. His eyes are the light. His face is in shadow. His hair's a wild mess beneath his cap.

"Help me?" he asks, stretching his hand out, and I bend over the sill and reach with all my height.

"I'm not tall enough," I say.

"Try harder."

I stand on my toes, press my knees into the low wall beneath the sill. I tip across the ledge, lower my shoulders, and now when Joey stretches, his hands clasp mine and he pulls himself toward me on the tree.

"Little by little," he says, his words pressed out of a too-small space, and I'm pulling so hard that I can't speak. "Slow," he says now, "and easy," and my arms are around him, his weight is near, I can hear his thumping heart, and the limb bends and rises like a seesaw game and the leaves shower down to the ground.

"It's not safe," I say.

"I'm almost there."

"The tree's not strong enough."

"It better be."

I hold tight and ease him in, hug him slow off the wobble of the tree—his cheek on my cheek now, his words in the space between my neck and chin. "Not bad for a girl," he says, and then he's laughing, and I'm laughing, pulling him up and in, until his head and neck and shoulders are through the open window, and his one knee is on the sill, and then the other is through, and he's beside me, in my house, in my attic, breaking every single rule, the splinters shivering beneath us.

"What are you doing?" I ask him, breathless.

"Aunt Cloris made cookies," he says. "Thought you should have some." And now he digs into his pocket and finds the cookie crumbs and puts the cookie back together on his hand.

"Chocolate chips," I say.

"That's right," he says, and then he's kissing me, breathless, and the cookie falls to the floor, and it's all I've ever wanted is these kisses.

"You shouldn't be here," I manage between everything.

"I should be," he says, "because I like you."

"I have brothers I never met," I tell Joey later, after the moon has decided to come out after all, a bright moon, growing smaller.

"Aunt Cloris told me," he says. "At least a little."

We lie each on one joist, the carpet of pink stuff between us, watching the moon disappear, the night grow lighter. "You'll get in trouble," I told him, but he said that he wouldn't, that Miss Cloris and Miss Helen were all in favor of keeping a friend in need safe.

"I've been safe all these years on my own," I told him.

"But now you don't have to be," he answered, and after that he held my hand over the fluff of pink stuff and stopped talking. We had a million things to say and nothing needing immediate saying. I had stories in my head—my

stories, his. I had his hand in my hand, the taste of Miss
Cloris's cookies on my lips, my mother sleeping down
below, the box of personals. There were two little boys.
They weren't outside. The fire got them. The fire still burns
my mother's knees. *What do you suppose any of us wish to
be remembered for?* she asked me. *For the things that tried
to stop us or the ways we carried on?*

"What are you going to do?" Joey asks me now.

"Find out the truth."

"What happens if you don't like the truth?"

"It can't be helped. It will be true."

"What are you hoping?"

"Hoping to stay here, to stop moving. To go to a real
school. To go into town. To get a dog of my own and take an
Airstream adventure." To go fly a kite, I almost say, but I
remember not to.

"That old Airstream," Joey says softly. "It's not going
anywhere."

"How do you know?"

"Because Aunt Helen's time is soon. She's dying, Sophie."

I turn, search for Joey's eyes in the dark. "She's dying
for sure?"

"Little by little, but quickly. Aunt Cloris pretends like
it's not going to happen. Aunt Helen lets her. It's the only
way, I guess, for them. Except sometimes I find Aunt Cloris
crying."

"How long," I ask, "does she have to live?"

"She stopped going to doctors," Joey says, "a year ago. She said there was nothing they could tell her that she didn't already know. Make every day count, is what she says now." I squeeze Joey's hand and close my eyes, try to picture Miss Cloris and Miss Helen. The big one and the little one. The wheeled chair and the custard. The clanking chains of the porch swing at night. Miss Cloris left behind. My whole body hurts just thinking of it. A tear falls from my eye, and then another tear, and now my whole face is drowning with the sadness of what is to come and what can't be changed and the pressing down of time.

"You're lucky," I say. "Growing up with them."

"I still miss my sister," he says. "And my mom and dad."

"Unlucky and lucky," I say. "At the same time."

Emmy

"'The barn was very large,'" I read, from the *Charlotte's Web* book. "'It was very old. It smelled of hay and it smelled of manure. It smelled of the perspiration of tired horses and the wonderful sweet breath of patient cows. It often had a sort of peaceful smell—as though nothing bad could happen ever again in the world.'"

Past the rectangle of the window, snow falls, fat and wet and white. All morning, all afternoon, it has laid its whiteness down, and beyond the window, in the courtyard, the bare trees wear the red bulbs of Christmas. The sound of the weather has worked its way inside—the hush-pause and the down tick, the ache in the clock on the walls.

"Autumn." I stop. "Sweetheart, look."

But she has closed her eyes and she won't look up. "Keep reading," she says with a sigh.

"'It smelled of grain and of harness dressing and of axle grease and of rubber boots and of new rope,'" I read on. "'And whenever the cat was given a fish-head to eat, the barn would smell of fish. But mostly it smelled of hay, for there was always hay in the great loft up overhead. And there was always hay being pitched down to the cows and the horses and the sheep.'"

I smell Christmas Eve on Autumn's breath, the chicken potpie that we ate with a slender wedge of cheese and a little puddle each of cranberry juice poured out in Dixie cups. Someone had brought in an old stereo and plugged it in with old-fashioned Christmas blues, and we sat there, together, while Jimmy Butler sang "Trim Your Tree" and Felix Gross sang "Love for Christmas," and when Sugar Chile Robinson sang "Christmas Boogie," Wolfie took up Virgin Mary's hand in hers and a space was cleared on the tabletop and the two of them danced, Virgin Mary's eyes a million miles away, but something close and near on her lips, something like a blessing. I half expected Autumn to dance, but she has learned her lesson, she says, or so she told Bettina five days ago, when they returned privileges to her and unlocked the door and told her, "But we are watching."

"'The barn was pleasantly warm in winter when the animals spent most of their time indoors,'" I continue, even though we both already know what will happen with the spider and the pig, the words in the web, the radiant, the terrific, the humble, "'and it was pleasantly cool in summer when the big doors stood wide open to the breeze.'"

"I'd like some of that summer breeze," Autumn says.

I take my time reading—give Charlotte A. Cavatica and

the farm fair and the magnum opus all the space they need, until my eyes start to close and my thoughts drift off to Baby and how I will not be holding her, will not be singing to her, will not be saying, "Happy First Christmas, Baby." I won't be saying, "I love you," and that is why she'll never know. You are not a mother if your daughter never knows.

I hear a knock at the door, the knob turn. "Bettina?" I say.

"Am I interrupting?" she asks, and when she comes in and stands there, I think of how Bettina is practically an inmate, too—born here or not, here she is, the Christmas hour approaching, and nowhere to go but to Room 433. She has let her hair grow down to her shoulders, and it falls in irregular curls. She has taken the cross from her neck and pulled a sweater over her uniform, and at the hem, some of her yellow slip sticks out. Her hose are white and see-through. Her knees look blue and cold.

I watch her watching me, just standing there, thinking something I can't see, and then it's as if she remembers why she's come, and from her apron pocket she slides a package tied with string. "It appears that you have a correspondent," she tells me, and I shake my head no. I have no correspondent. I have nothing, except for Autumn, except for Charlotte and Wilbur and the farm.

But she stands there anyway, lit up by the lamp beside her and the Christmas colors from the courtyard below. "Here," she says. "Addressed to you." I sit tall, my back against the wall, and the package smells like rainwater and stamp glue, wood shavings and graphite, the accordion fold of old air.

"Ma'am?"

"Yes?"

"I have no correspondent."

"Apparently, Emmy, you do."

I turn the packet over in my hands. Loosen the strings with my thumb. Look up at Bettina, but she only shrugs.

"Special delivery," she says, and she stands there waiting for me to open the thing, but I won't do that until she's gone.

"Merry Christmas," I say.

"Merry Christmas, Emmy, Autumn," she says after a minute goes by, after the snow keeps falling past the window. When the door closes, Autumn turns and sits up beside me, and still I hear Bettina in the hall, feel her near, smell her sadness, and I wish I had a present to give her, a box for her to take down the hall, to the elevator, past the guard, across the spokes, through the arch, into her quarters. If she was born here or not. If she is in love or never will be.

"What do you suppose?" she says.

"Don't know."

I set Charlotte aside. I slide the package from one hand to the other, turn it over again, do not recognize the handwriting on the brown envelope, cannot read the ink across the stamps. It is not a book, or I would feel it. It is not a hat; my mother's gone. It is not a scarf or mittens, because it has no lean into or stretch. It's something solid inside. Too hard and heavy to be fragile.

"Autumn," I say. "We are remembered."

The snow is falling. The year is almost done. I cannot see the clock on the wall or hear its ticking. I split the package seam with my longest finger, run my flesh through the thick packing, reach inside, and take my Christmas. It is cold to the touch; it is sculpted. It is driving wheels and bell and smokestack, cylinders and steam chest, whistle. I know what it is, and it is perfect.

"Who?" Autumn asks.

"Arlen," I say, and I am like the snow, falling, falling.

Sophie

❖　　　❖　　　❖　　　❖

He leaves the way he came—a shimmy down the long arms of the tree. I hear his front door swish and creak closed, and he is gone, and the light leaking in through the window is pink. From another rooftop or another tree, the crows return. I smell like Joey and attic splinters and chocolate.

Mother will wake soon. She'll rub her knees and call my name, and if I'm not where I'm supposed to be, there will be questions; there will be trouble. Slowly, I walk the attic boards and the right part of the stairs. I step into my room, change into a T-shirt. I crawl into bed and try to sleep over the wildness and strange hurt of my head.

When I wake, she is standing above me, her long hair falling forward. The sun through the window catches a small square of her face—the blue river of a vein working its way to her eye. The flesh beneath her lashes looks like the scratched-out scribble of a sketch.

"What's gotten into you?" she's asking.

"Mother?"

"Nine a.m. and still in bed?"

"It just happened," I say, rising up on my elbows and rubbing the sleep from one eye. My head still hurts, and now my heart, too, and my throat is like a scene from Cather's desert. I swallow and hear the click.

She studies me, tucks her hair behind her ears. She fits her hands onto her corduroy-skirt hips and leans in, closer. I take a long, deep breath and pray that she cannot hear my heart. "What's this?" she asks me now, lifting a spot of pink fluff out of my hair, into her hand.

"I don't know," I say, my heart so crazy that I'm sure she'll hear the wild thrash of it now, the bad inside it, the fear.

"Where did it come from?"

I shrug, lean away from her stare. "From cleaning?" I say, the first lie that comes to mind.

"From cleaning what, Sophie?"

"From behind the curtains, maybe? From when I was dusting your salts and peppers?"

"Those curtains are blue."

"I don't know," I say. "I really don't."

She balances the pink on the palm of her hand and lifts it higher, as if it's some formula she's captured, a new Archimedean solid. "Odd," she says now. "Very." In a cold, shattering voice that decides nothing. I turn and curl my knees toward my chin. I close my eyes as if I'm considering more sleeping. I feel the touch of her finger on my shoulder.

"No more," she says, "of that. The day has started."

"Okay."

"I'm going out, but not for long. We're short on supplies."

I stay still, not speaking.

"Sophie?"

"Yes?"

"I want you out of this bed and up and ready."

"Mother?"

"We'll have work to do when I get back."

I nod.

"And take a shower," she says. "You're smelling funny."

I run the loud center of the stairs and down into the front room. I tear through the kitchen, past the sinking icosahedron, into the laundry room, past the machines. My shampooed hair sits heavy on the bones of my shoulders. My sweatshirt falls baggy past my waist. The door to the basement rasps at its hinges and sucks at the air, and the web above my head floats loose.

I take the stairs one plank at a time, turn the square corner, see the dolls and the cars and the toys and the first box, flat as a brown carpet—everything as I left it, a dangerous wreck. There's no time for fixing. There's only time for my mother's second box of personals, which sits on the shelf above the ghost of the first—a Magnavox box with the FRAGILE signs pointing up, and the brown tape more shiny and steadfast. I pull it toward me, tug at the first loose tab of tape that I find. The cardboard tears; a seam pops. I dig my fingers under the second line of tape, and the box gapes, and my head hurts, and I catch my breath, knowing that I can stop this if I want to. I can still not know, can still be half of good, can not break this rule, not know these secrets.

But it's too late, too far. There was an attic and a window and acorns going splat. There was a boy with a ball and a dog, two aunts. There was my inside and their inside and all I never knew and all I ever wanted, and now I'm here, my knees sunk to the cool of the basement floor, my hands pulling at the box flaps, my lungs sucking in all the air they can hold, to power up my heart. I find scrapbooks, baby books, a curl of soft, blond hair. I find photographs and a puzzle board—the wooden shapes of hats and shoes. I find tiny hangers for tiny dresses and an orange tin of buttons and one yellow sock and Candy Land pieces and a photograph of my cat Chap and a felt bag of blocks and books never returned to the library after all, books still in their shiny, crackling covers, and a book of her own, *The Book of Thoughts.* I find toy tops and toy bananas and toy purses and plastic lipstick and a pair of train tickets and a pair of big shades and an umbrella no bigger than a doll would hold and a second photograph of Chap. My mother's second box of personals is the history of me—as if I am alive but the past of me isn't, as if everything I came from is part of shame or hush. I feel a hot, heaving sickness in my gut. I feel my mind too heavy with mystery to understand. To know what it means, to take it all in, to be here by myself. *Maybe we should come with you*, Miss Cloris said, and I'm wishing that I'd let her, that I wasn't here alone, that I had other people's courage with me, and other people's knowing.

"Sophie," I hear now. "You down there?"

"Mother?" I call up. My heart stops.

The top light snaps on and the door rasps and I hear Mother take one wobbling step down onto the plank. "What in the world," she's asking, "are you doing down here?" and there are stones in her voice, a cold coldness. I take *The Book of Thoughts* and stuff it up beneath my sweatshirt, spring from my knees. I hurry over cars and dolls, run up the stairs, stand on the square turn, halfway.

"I was looking for the broom," I say, and even I can hear how thin and breathless I sound, how unreliable. "The one with the dustpan."

"But the broom's up here," she says tightly. "In the closet."

"I guess I forgot," I say, certain that she can hear my tumbling heart from where she's standing, can see the thickness of things beneath my sweatshirt, can guess at how frightened I am that she will try to move past me—turn the corner, look down, see what I've done.

"What has gotten into you, Sophie Marks?" she demands. She holds herself steady with both of her hands, one fist each around the railing above the planks. The spiderweb trembles with every word she speaks. She glances up, then glances back down, looks into me.

"I wanted to clean," I tell her, and it's like the truth, all of a sudden, as if she has no right to doubt me, as if the only lies between us are her lies, stuffed into boxes.

"You already cleaned."

"But not with the broom," I say. "And I couldn't find it."

"Now, isn't that odd?" she says, and she stares at me for the longest time, black heat in her dark eyes and hurt in the way she stands, and suddenly I realize that she's tipping back, that she's losing balance, that she might stand on these steps and fall.

"Mother!" I call, and by the time I run the planks, she has tumbled to the landing—fallen back instead of forward, a shuddering sound that breaks the web from the rafters and sends it drifting into my arms, reaching for her.

"Now look what you've done," she says, pushing me away and steadying herself, looking hurt and small and full of indecision, as if she can't decide what to believe and she cannot keep her balance, and I feel sorry, all of a sudden—sorry for her knees, sorry for her hiding, sorry that she does not choose to trust me. That my past is not my past, but hers. That every single day she's been lying.

"Mother."

"The groceries," she says, pulling herself up now, so slowly by the thin rails of the basement, with the white fists of her hands. "Would you mind putting them away? I've left them on the counter." Her words are stiff and far away. She looks unwell and dizzy.

"Yes, ma'am."

"We don't need that kind of cleaning."

"Okay."

"When you're finished, you come and find me."

Emmy

When I wake, Autumn's gone. I don't need to open my eyes to know it. It's how the air feels less alive. It's how I am the only one who's breathing. It's what I don't smell, and what I do smell, which is fear.

"Autumn?" I say. "Autumn?" I yank the thin sheets off, pull my sweater from the drawers, see how the globe and the goggles have gone missing, how Autumn's bed is rumpled, empty. Autumn! I reach for the lamp and pull the chain, and in the hard light I see the note she's left me, written across the chest of drawers with a crayon stolen from Crafts. *Emmy, I will find him. He will help us.*

I turn, and there's the train on the sill. I tear through the sheets, through the drawers, but the envelope's gone, Arlen's address and handwriting, and Autumn is gone, and it is not yet dawn. "Autumn!" I cry, and I am across the room and through the door and running, my good leg, my bad leg, my feet bare, the sound of my weight on the tiles. It's dark and empty in the long hall, and only Julius is here, running his mop across the floor. "You see her?" I ask him, and he shakes his head no, and still I'm running, calling her name, banging my hand against

the red down of the elevator button—one two three four
five one two three—until it pings and the doors glide open,
glide closed. Four. Three. Two. One. When the door pings
open again, I run down the long hall past the pale windows,
past the courtyard, which is piled high with snow. "Autumn!"
I call, and the guard at the front desk is sound asleep over his
Daily News, his feet up on the desk, his head thrown back, as
though somebody went and put pills in his cup. Somebody
could have. *I have him under my spell.* Autumn? I remember the
globe of pills. I think of her note upstairs. I think of Autumn
wanting to be free every single day. And with every second
that passes, the sun is rising, and through the door now, the
heavy panels of glass, I see footprints, fresh, in the snow,
across the spoking paths. I see the scarf, a slash of red, against
the white.

"Autumn!" I cry, and the guard doesn't stir. I reach the
door. I yank it hard. And I am running.

Sophie

"She found you?" Joey's saying. "When you were down there?"

"Never been so scared."

"And then she fell? Backward?"

"Like she was fainting, but she wasn't. She was all down on the floor and then all come-to, telling me to put the groceries away, and then to go find her, and when I found her, she was on the La-Z-Boy, and she wouldn't look up; she wanted nothing. She'd been to the library, and the old books were gone—all the math and science. She was fast asleep. She's sleeping now."

"You sure?"

I nod, trace my fingers down the long scratch of Joey's arm, a twig scratch, wrist to elbow. He has leaves in his hair, like he is wearing a costume, instead of the cap he mostly keeps on his head, and he called me Rapunzel when he climbed inside, and then he leaned down and he kissed me, the salt and sweet of peanuts, long and out of breath from all the climbing, the reaching for me and me for him, and then he remembered that he'd brought me a brownie, which was Ziplocked in his pocket and shaped like squish from the climb. "They're sending their love," he said, and then he said that he couldn't stay long, and besides, he was afraid of my mother waking up and climbing the stairs, and everything he said, he said in a whisper, which is harder than talking and more tiring, too.

"Couldn't ever make it up those attic stairs," I promise. I whisper, too. I know the risks we are taking.

"But what if she hears us?"

"I'll say it's mice that I was chasing."

"You have it all planned out?"

"Contingencies," I tell him, sounding braver than I feel. "The old what-ifs."

"I guess."

He stands there, balanced on his attic plank, tall, with pitcher's arms and curly, leaf-stuck hair. I stand here, two feet on my plank, in worn-down jeans, my sweatshirt strings too tight at my neck. When Joey leans, I lean and his lips are mine, his breath is my breath is his breath. "Share it?" I ask, pulling back, meaning the brownie, but he says he's had plenty already, and dinner is soon, besides, and when I pull the squish from the Ziploc and break a piece and put it on my tongue, it's a beautiful melting moistness like none I've ever had.

"I found something," I say when my tasting and swallowing is done.

"What did you find?"

"*The Book of Thoughts*. In the personals. In the basement." I rustle my hand up into the folds of my sweatshirt and pull the book into the light that comes in through the window. It's a thin paper thing, hardly any writing to it. I flip through it, then snap it shut, and close my eyes, and keep breathing.

"It's five sentences," I say. "Or six."

"That all? That's all her thoughts?"

"I'm not really sure," I say. "Exactly. Some of her thoughts. I guess. At least."

"Looks old," Joey says, looking from me to the book, which I've placed on the sill. "And rained on."

"Box has got a date on it," I say. "November 1995."

"At least that old, then."

"At the very least."

"What else was in there?"

"Photographs. Baby toys. Little plastic hangers. Juggling puzzle pieces."

"That all?"

"Didn't have time but to grab one thing."

"*The Book of Thoughts,*" he says.

"Would you read it?"

"Me?"

"The way you read to Miss Helen?"

"Right here? Like this?"

I reach to pull a leaf from his hair. I reach again to kiss him. "I'd feel better," I say, "hearing it from you."

"All right," he says, leaning closer.

I trade my plank for his and crush beside him.

"*'The Book of Thoughts*,'" he reads. "Page one. 'We love in our own ways.'"

"That's all of page one?"

"That's all she put there."

He reads the way he reads.

I close my eyes to listen.

The Book of Thoughts

We love in our own ways.

The sky was blue, and it was easy.

I wanted to die. They wouldn't let me. I wanted home. There was no home. And after that, when it was done, after it all, then I had nothing. We love, and it's gone up in smoke.

There was no one who could understand. I went from town to town, then stopped. I worked the Clock and Watch. I took my hour off ahead of noon and walked the back streets, empty, and the sun was a flame, and it was the fault of the streets being empty. It was the fault of whoever had left you. It was the fault of them not knowing that children left untended die. I worked the Clock and Watch. I was walking the neighborhood streets, which were sun-blazed and empty. Your hands in the grass were pale and pudgy. You had been left to the weather.

I wore white, a mother's color. The sky was blue, and it was easy.

We love in our own ways.

Emmy

☙   ☙   ☙   ☙

I ran where she had run. I fit my footprints into hers—down the stairs, across the courtyard path, between the benches piled with snow and the half-wall of azaleas, like animals with crystal fur, past the red jag of the scarf in the snow. The end of the night was the beginning of day. The sky was fuzzy. Now the footpath was Carter Road, and the road turned, and to one side was the brick face of a long, low building, the black spirals of escape stairs, the smoking chimneys, and to the other was the wild slope of iced grass and white stones. Beyond the field was the dark hem of far trees, and hanging from the limbs of the trees were bottles and cans catching glints from the sun that was still rising.

"Autumn!" I kept calling. "Autumn!" Her name freezing in the air before me, then snapping back. My bad leg was a thin pole. My feet were blue in the snow. "Autumn!" Her note in my pocket, her words in my head, her practicing—our practicing—to be free. And now the narrow road turned, and the plowed snow was banked to either side, and the highway was up ahead. In the dawn before me was the globe. Africa, North America, Asia, the constellation of spilled pills—how many, I wondered, had she slipped into the guard's cup, and how, *how* had she done it?—and still the footsteps were running between the treads of tires in the snow. I could hear a bus chuffing up ahead, the honk and blare of cars in a hurry to get anywhere but State. I could smell the burn of tires against the slick of snow, the fumes burning through, and I knew before I got there, before I saw the long, angry knot of traffic, the rounding red and blue of the police cars, the hard heart of the ambulance, with its doors slamming closed. "Autumn!" I was screaming. "Autumn!" And she was locked inside, and the siren lit up, and she was gone. There was a man and a woman, a car pulled to one side, its headlight shattered. There were the goggles, where she'd dropped them, to the ground.

Emmy, I will find him. He will help us.

"No! No! No!" I screamed. But the ambulance drove off, and Autumn was gone.·

Sophie

"There's something else," Joey says, and he's holding me now, both his arms around me, his back against the wall, my back into him, and in his hands a page of yellowed newsprint that had fallen from *The Book of Thoughts* to the fluffed-pink floor.

"I don't understand," I say over the hard knuckle of my throat, and he hugs me for a long time and says nothing, and now he turns the newsprint in the square of window sun and reads: "'Infant Stolen in Broad Daylight.'" There's a picture of a baby. There's the baby's mother, her eyes round and big like the baby's. "Manhunt Continues," the smaller headline reads. "Mrs. Rane could not be reached for comment."

Emmy

❦   ❦   ❦   ❦

She stands too straight in the spine, as though she is stacked inside with secrets. She folds and crouches close.

"There is news," Bettina says.

I turn in my bed and say nothing. I stare at her through the glass of my eyes. She has come every night, so many nights, since Autumn died, her goggles the only important something she left behind. She has come again tonight, claiming news. She reaches for my hand. I let her take it. She wears her cross again, touches it with her free fingers, stares into the night, into the wild and ruined world.

The night is shiver cold. The air is crystals. Bettina pulls the blanket to my chin.

Autumn never told me her secret, I want to say. I must confess. I cannot bear it. Because it was my secret that stole her, that took her from me; her cot is empty.

"We have had our conference, Emmy," Bettina says now, after so much silence has passed between us. "We are agreed."

"You are agreed," I repeat, the words dull in my mouth.

"Dr. Brightman will meet with you tomorrow. He'll explain." She exhales, and the air goes white.

"Explain what?" I ask.

"Impeccable behavior. Consistent self-care. Responsible. Trustworthy. No episodes. I wrote a report. Miss Banks wrote a report. Even Granger wrote a report. Dr. Brightman has been watching, and he listened."

I shake my head, don't understand.

"Your freedom, Emmy."

"My freedom?"

"There'll be rehabilitation, of course," she says. "Steps to take. A process. But you'll be free. They will release you. You will have your old life back."

"I will never have my old life back."

"You have earned your wings."

"Listen to me," I say. "Listen. I have got no place to go. What good is releasing?"

"You will make your own home, Emmy. You'll be taught how. You'll get a job. Vocational will help you."

"But," I say.

"This is an opportunity," she says.

And she holds my hand, holds it like Mama would have.

"My heart is broke," I say.

Sophie

The knock comes in the middle of the night and keeps on coming—a smash against the door, a pounding like an animal running. "Cheryl Marks," the voice calls. "Open up." And I can hear Mother in her room, creaking off her bed, creaking on the floorboards, her bad leg dragging. "Jesus," I hear her saying. "Oh, sweet Jesus." And now she's calling to me in an edge of broken whisper, "You keep to yourself, Sophie. You let me handle this." And still she's walking in circles, dragging her leg, and the smashing comes faster, harder, and they'll break the door to nothing; they will bang through it, blow the house down, and Mother's on the stairs calling, "I'm coming," in her best official voice. "I'm coming." She walks the loud middle of the steps, turns the corner on the landing, and when she descends again, takes the last flight of stairs down, I crawl from my bed and head to my door and go as far as I can without her seeing, my head hanging over the rail now as she drags across the living-room floor. The banging stops, and the mix-up of voices, and now there's the flame of flashlights against the back wall, a spiking flicker that slowly settles until the downstairs is aglow, and my mother's shadow and their shadows bulge and shrivel on the illuminating wall, and Miss Cloris is among them. It's her square shadow. It's her puffs of hair, her shape behind the others. There are three of the others, and there is my mother, and there is Miss Cloris, and my mother is screaming, "Don't touch me!" and the voices, the men, are saying, "Calm yourself, Mrs. Marks. We have some questions."

"*You* have some questions?" she shouts back. "Barging in here in the middle of the night?"

"It has come to our attention."

"What has?"

"We are speaking of a serious crime."

"Sleeping in one's own house is a crime?"

"If you'd just come with us, down to the station."

"I have work. The first shift. In the morning."

"Mrs. Marks."

And now there's the shuffling of paper, and one of the men walking toward her, and now she's growling, "Where did you get that? Wherever did you . . . ?" Her voice like a knife scraping a plate, and I think of Joey, scrambling down the tree, *The Book of Thoughts* tucked into his shirt, the stolen infant, the promises he was making—"They'll know what to do; they always do." And I think of my mother, at dinner tonight, the long sorrow in her eyes and the thieving in her and her not knowing that I was knowing, that

Joey'd read her words: *The sky was blue, and it was easy. We love in our own ways.* "What's the matter with you?" my mother demanded, impatient. "You aren't eating, and it's store-bought, too." And I couldn't breathe, and I couldn't swallow, and I held my hand against my chest, so that all the broken pieces of my heart wouldn't bleed the space between us. *The No Good is you,* I wanted to say. *You running from you, you taking me with you.* And it was right here all along, and if white is a mother's color, what is my mother wearing? Where is she—my real, true mother? *Be good.*

"Calm yourself, Mrs. Marks," they're saying. "We'd like to take you downtown, ask you some questions." But she's growling at them now. She's kicking and I see it all in the spike lights on the wall, see the biggest man of the three taking her elbow into his hand, and the other coming up to her other side, and Mother insisting, "You ask me right here," and someone saying, "You have the right . . ." And all this time, Miss Cloris is a tilted shadow on the wall, and finally it's Miss Cloris who says, "Let's not forget what is most important here." My mother is being wrestled down. There's the sound of chains and key, and she's growling, my mother, demanding to know who Miss Cloris is and what she's speaking of and is she the owner of the infernal dog and if there's any trouble on this street, it starts with that wolf barker, and over this and through it, Miss Cloris is saying, "Let's not forget why we are here. The child's name is Sophie."

"There is no such thing," my mother spits. "No such one." And the men hold her back, and the blare lights tangle, and I am going to be sick. I'm going to throw up on the floor, and suddenly I hear a long terrible howling, worse than animal, worse than jungle, or Mother, and it is my own stolen self, and I am ashamed, found out, and I can't stop howling.

"Will someone let me through!" Miss Cloris is saying, "For God's sake, she is a child." And now I hear her wide feet on the stairs and her, breathless, coming for me, and I feel her arms around me, her hands in my hair. "Sophie. Love." And it's all I can do to lift my arms up to her, to let her hold me, to take every ounce of goodness from her, which is every square and cell.

"Miss Cloris," I sob, and she says, "I know, my love."

And I say, "But I was stolen from."

And she says, "It isn't right. But we're here now. We're here to help you."

Emmy

The snow has piled high; the earth is wet. The sun has come in on the horizon. On the walk below, a robin shrugs the white fluff from her wings, and a squirrel sits twitching its tail. Behind me, on Cot A, my bags are packed—the Levis I arrived with, the yellow sock, Autumn's goggles and Autumn's globe, because now Autumn's things are mine. "It's your time," Bettina said. But I don't understand time anymore.

Out there, beyond, the mail truck pulls into Administration, and a car winds down Carter Road. Out there the sun paints a stripe of gold down the sheer icicles. Out there, somewhere, is Baby. *Psshhhahh,* I think, wiping a tear from my face, and now, overhead, a gang of fat geese fly—heavy, lifted, hollering geese—and I follow their trail with my eye. "Your chunk of sky," I say to Autumn, and I feel a breeze blow by.

"Emmy?" It's Bettina at the door. "You coming?"

"I'm coming," I say. "I will."

"You forget something, you can come back for it later."

"I'm not forgetting," I tell her. "I swear."

Sophie

❈   ❈   ❈   ❈

There was talk for a long time. There were police rooms and courtrooms and a lady testing my head and a lady testing my heart, which was a million shattered pieces. I don't know how you live with so many shattered pieces. There was a dentist who said my teeth were the whitest he'd ever seen for someone who'd gone untended. There was a doctor measuring me to the seventy-fifth, checking every part that makes me whole, and you are whole, they kept saying. It is amazing, they said, above my head. There were social workers and therapists and so many people asking questions, and Miss Cloris never left me, or her lawyer, either, a nice old man in a charcoal suit who claimed to be Miss Cloris's brother-in-law. "You have a sister with a husband?" I asked, trying to follow. "I have an ex-husband with a brother," she answered, and she was unlocking the Airstream just then, walking me in, saying it was mine for as long as I would need it, that the system agreed, that we had won, at least, that battle, and I didn't ask questions because there were already too many questions, too many things I couldn't make sense of. My mother is in lockup;

her trial's coming. The house where I lived is evidence. The boxes of personals have been packed by the experts and shipped to a lab far from here—the little cars, the plastic men, the photographs, the yellow sock, the hangers that are the size I was then, and around whatever is left is the sticky caution tape, which flaps in the wind and doesn't break in the storms and tells everybody who drives by slow where the problem was, what the news is. "She is not talking to anyone," Miss Cloris said for me. No one in trucks and no one with cameras and no one with microphones, until finally they let us alone, because you can't get past Miss Cloris. You can't be built like she is, her size and her shape, and think she's going to give in to something you're asking. "She's just a child," she'll say into the phone. And then she'll hang it up loud, bang it to its cradle, and invite me to her table for tea, and we will sit there, the two of us, in the middle of the morning, and try to make sense of right now and also try to get ready for the future.

Miss Helen's sick, but she will not see a doctor—"Let it be," she says. "Let it be." Joey reads when he's home and Minxy watches and sometimes in the afternoons I learn to throw better than a girl; I learn to lean harder on Joey, and he lets me. He lets me talk when I have to and stop when I can't, and sometimes he tells me the story, again, of how he survived, when his whole world crashed in, was robbed and stolen. And in the mornings, when Joey's gone, I leash

Harvey like Miss Cloris has taught me and take him on a walk and no one stops me; no one says, "Sophie, be good." The door slams and it is no secret. The door opens, and I'm home. The world is complicated, and I am, too, and Miss Cloris says that the only way to see the sky is to keep looking up, looking forward.

It's silver inside the Airstream, silver and old, with a pullout bed that's rounded at the edge and a string of clattery beads separating the bed from the toilet. Miss Helen's White Rabbit lives here—in the sheets, in the curtains, in the little welcome mat where I leave my shoes—and on the wall there's a photograph in a rounded silver frame: Miss Cloris and Miss Helen, walking hand in hand.

"That was before," Miss Cloris said when she saw me staring at it, "when Helen was strong."

"You're wearing a dress," I said.

"I am."

"You look better in pants."

She hugged me so hard I couldn't breathe.

They've searched for my parents, for the Mr. and the Mrs. Rane. They found my father dead. "It was an embolism," Miss Cloris told me. "Died at work, just twenty-seven." She sat beside me, on the silver bed, and gave me the news real slow, and I cried for a long time, for never having known my father, for never having had one, for being stolen away from the chance. Miss Cloris didn't pretend it was all right. She didn't say there, there. She let me cry until I was out of tears, and then she said you rest right here, and left the Airstream, and then she came back with a warmed-up slice of pie. "Blueberry," she told me, and then she went out to get me seconds, and after I was done, she took my hand and said, "They're still doing the detective on your mama."

But every day that goes by, my mama's missing, and every day, too, my mother sits in a prison where they say I should not see her, the fire in her knees, the dark in her eyes, the thieving, the Kepler she wouldn't believe in.

The sky was blue, and it was easy.

The archbishop has died, but the bell tolls for him, high above the streets of Santa Fe, and his church, Miss Helen says, stands tall and actual. Miss Cloris cried at the end— cried hard and we didn't try to stop her—and Joey closed his eyes, and it wasn't but for a few days later when Miss Helen suggested that we move on to poems. Short packages, she called them. Tied up with meaning. And every now and then I'll read, and when I look up, Miss Cloris is crying.

Monday through Friday, Joey's at school. Monday through Friday, one o'clock, my tutor comes, Miss Mandy Stanley, her blond hair straight and smooth to her shoulders, her eyes like gem rocks widely broken. She brings me lessons about notebooks and homework. Lessons about keeping organized. We fit tabbed paper between lined paper and snap the notebooks shut, and we fill index cards with the notes we take from the textbooks we are reading. "You'll be ready come January," she tells me every day, and I say that if that happens, then I'll miss her, and if that happens, also, I will not know what to do. I will not know how to walk the corridors of a school and pack up when the bell rings and fiddle the numbers on my locker and put my money out for the cafeteria food—and Miss Mandy and me, we talk it through. "Don't you ever underestimate your own intelligence," she says when I start worrying down my list of worries, and I want with my whole heart to believe like Miss Mandy does, to see the world like she does, through those eyes.

"Sophie?" Miss Cloris calls me now. "You in there?" She taps at the Airstream door the way she does, with the side of her ring-finger knuckle.

"I am."

"You be ready in an hour?"

"I will." Because today is Joey's birthday, and he's hookying off of school, and the wind is kicking high and the clouds beyond the Airstream windows are sailing loose and woolly. It's like a day rinsing clean, and I have tied my hair up in a high ponytail and put on my best dress and slipped Miss Helen's beaded purse across my shoulder, a little square hung from a string. It smells like mint and tea leaves and the nub of old lipstick. And when I step outside, I stand straight as I can. Stand like Miss Cloris says to stand, which is tall enough and straight enough that I can see the sky.

An hour later, we're in Miss Cloris's old Civic—Miss Helen with Miss Cloris up front and me and Joey in the back, holding hands, and Harvey left at home, barking at us through the window. "You're in charge now," Miss Cloris told him as she locked the door, and then we drove off, down the street, around the bend, to the bigger road against which the big buildings sit—the library, the post office, Hanover's Foods, my mother's diner. Miss Cloris drives slow—"We're special cargo," she says—and even if some people honk or wave their hands or make their funny faces, we don't mind, because it is Joey's day and not one of us has told him the surprise.

When we get to a gravel wedge by the side of a smaller road, Miss Cloris parks and I make Joey close his eyes and Miss Helen promises to sit right with him, on guard, while Miss Cloris and I unpack the Civic's trunk and carry the all of it—the baskets and blanket and kite in a sack, the pitcher of raspberry lemonade—to a smooth face of rock that Miss Cloris remembers. By the third trip back to the Civic, through the tall grass and the weeds, we are ready. Miss Cloris scoops Miss Helen into her arms. I lead

Joey, who hasn't opened his eyes, who keeps a promise tight, who holds my hand like he will for all of time. We're alone out here. We're alone, and the wind is blowing.

In Miss Cloris's arms, Miss Helen and her green dress float like a leaf gotten loose on a stream. Beside me, Joey's cap is stuck backward; his long leather belt is softly slapping. Miss Cloris's shirttail hangs over a pair of pinstriped trousers, and now we're near to the rock and she turns and she says, "Aren't we a sight?" as if that's the best thing any whole person could say about another. I glance down at me—at the peach dress Miss Cloris and I bought at the store, at the ruby-beaded purse cutting crosswise from my shoulder. "We're a sight," I say, and then we're laughing, as if nothing was ever wrong or ever could be, as if we engineered goodness. As if we have that power.

There's the scurrying of animals we can't see, but we can hear them. There are deer way over, at the broad field's edge, and from the limbs of the trees at the edge of the field, old bottles are hung, like a crooked set of chimes. Above us, the sky is sketch and wings, and clouds roll back in, while far away, in the distance, an old building crumbles. Many buildings—tunnels and bridges, a wall of stone, and walls of brick, and roofs that are cracked, and big twiggy bushes that have been pulled up and piled to one side. "The old hospital," Miss Cloris says when I ask her. "Developers bought the land, but the buildings sit there, rotting."

"Why rotting?"

"Because sometimes it takes time," she says, "to scoop out the old and make new."

The whole thing is broken into. The outside stairs are springing off, like bad curls, and the brick is boned over by old ivy. There are sprays of paint across it all—red lions, a pair of blue horns, a silver graffiti chandelier. It's crumbled, tossed, and left behind, but there's a strange kind of beauty to it.

"Seems like a sad place," I say, and we just stand there looking until finally we remember that Joey has kept his eyes closed, that we're here for a performance, that we have practiced. It's Joey's birthday. It's Joey's day.

"Don't open them yet," I say, and behind Joey's back, Miss Cloris and I slip the kite from where it's been hiding in its Hefty. Together, while he waits, we untangle the string. Together, while Miss Helen smiles, we get ourselves ready. When there's nothing more to do, we look at each other, square in the eyes.

"It's your show," Miss Cloris says. "Do you hear me?"

She puts the kite in one of my hands and the ball of string in the other. She tells me to strike a bargain with the wind, to do as she has told me to do, when we were practicing this day for Joey. "Joey," she says now, "you can open your eyes," and all of a sudden, I'm running—across the sink and rise, through the weeds and grass, toward the crumble of the hospital, beneath sky. I'm running, and the kite is jostling behind. It tugs, and it kicks. It doesn't take flight.

"Keep going!" Miss Cloris yells, and I'm running.

"Faster!" Miss Cloris calls out. "Faster!" And now Joey is yelling with her, and Miss Helen is calling to give the kite more string, and when I glance back, I see Miss Cloris standing tall as a woman like Miss Cloris can stand and Joey taller beside her, Miss Helen on the blanket at their feet. "You're doing it," they're telling me. "You're putting on some show." And right at that moment, right when I lose all hope of magic, the electric orange of the kite goes zing and the string whips, slips, tightens, and when I look up, behind me, I see the kite going high, a red-tailed hawk swooping by.

Higher and higher goes the bright zinging kite, the collars and buttons and seams of its tail, the zippers and puff parts and dainty see-throughs. From far away, I hear Miss Cloris telling me to do as we planned to do, which is to say, let the kite go free. "Let it go," she calls. "Let it all be." And when I do, when the last final inch of the string burns through, when I am holding on to nothing but drawn-down bits of sky, I look up and see the kite float higher than the birds, toward the clouds that are rolling in, woolly. I hear the jangle of collars against zippers against seams, and now I hear a long whooping and hollering and I turn to see Joey running—through the tall grass down the hill, toward me. "Sophie!" he's calling. "Sophie!" And when he reaches me, I'm off the ground, Joey's arms lifting me skyward. "You fly a kite better than any girl ever," he's saying, breathless, and his lips are on mine. Far away, in the rock face of the old building, I hear echoes in pipes and old rainwater sponging through tiles. I hear the bark of a dog and the buzzing of insects, and I remember Miss Cloris's words about tragedy and happiness, and how sometimes the two are the same one thing, and I think of Cheryl Marks, her own No Good: *Seek perfection in all that you do.*

"Better than any girl ever?" I ask when the kiss is over, and Joey nods yes, and he takes my hand, and we start back up the long grass hill, and above us the sky is still brewing its storm, and by the time we reach the smooth rock, a gust has started to blow.

"We'll be drenched," Miss Cloris says, "if we wait any longer. We'll be drenched, and bless you, Sophie. You did fine." She lifts Miss Helen and her float of dress high. Joey and I gather every other last thing.

"Must the party be over?" Miss Helen asks, her voice a whisper.

"Can't afford to catch a cold, dear," Miss Cloris says,

hugging her tight, and we set off for the narrow strip of gravel.

They are there when we pull to the curb—the big man and the brother-in-law, and a couple beside them. They stand on the porch, taking shelter from the purple slash of rain that has come in hard in the last few minutes. Miss Cloris steers the car to a stop and lets the engine idle. She sits and she watches and waits. She turns around and studies me hard, then asks us, very quietly, very oddly demure, if we would all mind staying put for the moment. She opens her car door. She slams it shut. She hurries up the walk, a hand above her heart.

"Who are they?" I ask Joey, but he doesn't know and pulls me close, and the rain is falling too hard for me to hear what is said—the brother-in-law to Miss Cloris first, and then the big man to Miss Cloris, and then the woman and Miss Cloris talk while the last man paces, his hair like knitting yarn rubbed out in spots and his shoulders too small inside his sweater. But it's the woman I watch most closely, her blond hair against the slick white of her trench coat, the belt of her coat tied, not buckled. She wears plain tan boots that lace up past her ankles. The hem of a red skirt falls past her coat, and she moves from one foot to the other, her hands on the ends of her belt, her hands like birds, fluttering, worried.

"Who is *she*?" I ask, the words a jumble in my throat, and Miss Helen turns, her eyes full on me, her mouth making little marks against time but saying nothing, and now Joey pulls me even closer, holds me harder in the back of the car, and I can't breathe, but I have to breathe, and the woman turns, and she keeps turning, toward the steps and down and out, and now she runs. She is a ruin in the rain, she is a break against the purple slash, she is breaking and crying and running, her eyes a bright smash, her hands like small birds flying. "Baby," I hear her. "Baby. Baby." And the sky is not blue; it is not easy.

❊   ❊   ❊   ❊

Acknowledgments

This book began with an obsession concerning certain abandoned buildings and the lives of urban explorers. It took me to a place once known as Byberry, in the northeast corner of Philadelphia, and to the stories Jim Cuorato, Paul Lonie, and Dominic Ragucci told about a building that once was, about the patients who passed through.

Lauren Wein of Black Cat gave me cause to keep on writing; she believed in this story and my ability to make it whole; she sent e-mails that were full of graces, poetry. Marjorie Braman read twice with care, offered wisdom, and kept me company with stories of chocolates and flowers. And then, one summer day, Laura Geringer read and asked a question: What if? I am so deeply grateful.

Tremendous gratitude to Amy Rennert and her associate, Robyn Russell, who read this book throughout the three years of its making, who kept me grounded in a week of high panic, and who, with calm and wisdom, fell upon this novel's title.

Thank you to Mandy Stanley, whose gifts to me, and to the world, are innumerable. Thank you to Amy Riley, who discovered my work, three books ago, and generously, systematically, introduced me to her community of book-loving friends. Thank you to the book bloggers out there who have changed the way I think about the world and whose opinions and daring I treasure.

My thanks to Rahna Reiko Rizzuto and Ivy Goodman, dear friends who read quickly and who bolstered my long journey. My sincere thanks to Alyson Hagy, Elizabeth Hand, Jay Kirk, Katrina Kenison, Anna Lefler, Kate Moses, Jennie Nash, and Karen Rile, who bring crystal light into my life. Thank you to the remarkable Neil Swaab for a cover that is, in a word, perfect. My thanks to Elizabeth Mosier, who reads books through a brilliant lens, who throws parties with a book lover's grandeur, and who wrote words I will forever cherish.

This book is dedicated to the men in my life—to my artist husband, Bill, and to my son, Jeremy, who asks, nearly every single time he calls, for stories about the stories.

Finally, where would this book be without Egmont USA—that irreplaceable team of enthusiasts, intellects, and believers? Thank you, Elizabeth Law (might I now call you Lawsy?), Doug Pocock, Greg Ferguson, Mary Albi, Rob Guzman, Katie Halata, Alison Weiss, superb copyeditor Hannah Mahoney, and that master of case covers, Nico Medina. The world is a special place, thanks to you.